# TALK TO ME

To Glenn
who makes anything possible

# One

# SADINA

I turn around and Maddie is gone.

That's how it happens, that quickly. Things go wrong in the time it takes me to slide a set of headphones off my ears and turn around to hand them to Maddie. I'm listening to a CD in Playlist, the only music store in the mall, and there's this song I want her to hear, but she's gone.

Here's the thing with Maddie: I always know when she's near me, but it's never by the sound of her voice. In a place like this—a place with other people around, I mean—she doesn't talk at all. But I still hear the rubbery squeak of her pink sneakers a pace behind me, smell the candy-sweet scent of her shampoo, feel her fingertips brush against my palm even though—so she says—she's really too old to hold hands.

This time my senses have let me down. She's nowhere near me, and it takes me about twenty seconds to figure out that she's not in the store at all.

Rio must have seen something in my face. Suddenly he's by my side, exactly in the spot I expected Maddie to be.

"What's wrong?" he asks, but I don't even have to answer, because right away he registers that my little sister sidekick is not where she's supposed to be.

I know I should be sliding right into Emergency Procedure Plan A: if Maddie disappears, pull cord to release oxygen mask, cover mouth, assume crash position. Or maybe it's stop, drop, and roll. What am I supposed to be doing? Tell somebody, yell for help—but I can't seem to make myself move. Instead a million stupid thoughts are whirling in my head, like, *how can I possibly tell my mother I've lost Maddie? Why can't I have a little sister who's completely, boringly normal? How come I always have to play guardian angel? I never asked for the job.*

Rio, who knows me like a book he's read every day for ten years, watches me with narrowed eyes. This isn't the way it usually goes. Usually I'm the one who faces trouble by making noise, who pulls Rio out the door and into a thunderstorm when he'd rather be doing just about anything else. Usually I'm the monkey in the zoo who throws fruit at you through the bars of the cage and screeches right in your face. But this is different. This is about Maddie, my sweet silent sister. Now I stand without speaking, immobilized in a puddle of my own panic.

"Sadina, take it easy, we'll find her," Rio says. It's for himself as much as me. He loves Maddie too. He reaches out to touch my hand; I'm twirling a strand of hair tight around one finger. It's a baby habit, pulling on my own hair whenever I stress out, something I should have shaken off in first grade. Rio pulls my hair out of my hand and tucks it behind my shoulder, and just like that, with that one touch of ordinary, the regular me starts to seep back into place.

What the regular me thinks of is Mr. Jaworski, my math teacher, who always tells us, "Before you try to solve a problem, make sure you know what you're looking for." Well, that's easy. I'm looking for Maddie, my seven-year-old sister. But it's bigger than that. I'm looking for a seven-year-old girl who can't answer—maybe even can't make herself move—when I call her name.

"Come on, let's get security, they can search this whole place," Rio starts, and then trails off as I shake my head.

"No way, Rio. You know she won't answer them. They'll just scare her to death." I want to bite back that last word as soon as I say it. I imagine how her face looks right now, wherever she is, and my stomach gives a small sick jolt.

Rio puts his hand on my back and nudges me toward the store's exit. "Let's move. We're wasting time." His voice is rising, and I realize we're both balanced right on the outside edge of control. "Where's the last place you remember seeing her?"

Good question. One problem: I have no idea. Okay, deep breath. We can do this. We can retrace our steps. We'll find you, Maddie, I swear we'll find you.

"I don't know. I can't even remember the last place we've been. Wait—the toy store, maybe? She wanted to look at the Legos, right?"

If Rio answers, I never hear it. As I step out of the store an alarm shrieks out a warning. The noise is so loud it's a live thing, pulsing into my ears and pounding on me from the inside. I'm no good with loud noises: I shy from them like a dog from fire, and if this noise were a fire it would be an inferno, thousands of degrees past what I can take. My feet meld to the floor. Then Rio pulls me back into the store, and the blaring quits, and I can hear and think again.

Before I can even figure out what happened someone grabs me by the arm, hard, and puts his face right in mine.

"Where do you think you're going with that CD?" he says. I take in a narrow face that belongs to a tall guy in a Playlist shirt, with a nametag that says Store Manager. I look down at my hand and see that I'm still holding the CD, the one I wanted Maddie to hear. I must have tripped the alarm at the door. The CD is by Polite Convention, my favorite band, singing *talk to me, girl, your words are my house and my haven and my path to your heart* with the notes piled up so sweet and pure, I almost cried when I heard it.

"I didn't mean to take this…it's my sister, she's gone, I just noticed—I don't even want to buy this, I just wanted her to listen." Something's not clicking between my brain and my lips. The words are coming out garbled and even I can't make sense of them.

Store Manager guy looks at me like I'm already a felon. "I've been watching both of you since you walked in here. There wasn't anyone else with you." He flicks a hand toward the back of the store. "You just need to step over here while I call security."

"She wasn't stealing it," Rio breaks in. "Listen, she's telling the truth. Her sister's missing and we're trying to find her." I can't believe his voice is so calm, so reasonable and polite, when I can tell that he's two breaths from bursting. Rio shakes his dyed-black bangs out of his eyes and even manages a half-smile, the one he uses on his mother when he forgets to take out the garbage, stays out too late, wants a ride to the mall.

What melts Rio's mom doesn't impress Store Manager guy. People are starting to clump and stare, and it's clear he wants us out of the way. He gestures again to the back of the store.

If we go with him, it'll take forever to talk our way out of this. And every second that goes by is one more second of Maddie alone and scared. Rio looks at me sideways. It's the lay-it-on-the-line, jumping-off-a-cliff look he gets when he thinks he's out of options. I'm pretty sure I know what he's about to do. And I'm right. In one smooth motion he takes the CD from my hand, slaps it hard on a shelf, and pulls me from Store Manager's grip.

And we run.

# Two

# MADDIE

**M**addie sits in the corner with her back to the wall. She can think herself small as a kitten, small as a mouse. Just hold very still, so no one will see her. So no one will speak to her. That's the worst, the speaking. They come at her with words she can't answer, and her silence makes them spill out more words, filling the space around her so that she can hardly breathe. Sometime the words are as soft as pillows, placed at her feet like promises. Other times the words fly at her like darts, stinging her with their angry impatience. But it makes no difference. She can't answer any of them. Don't let the words find her. Just stay small. Just stay still.

# Three

# SADINA

It's three o'clock on a Sunday afternoon and the mall is packed. That works against us as much as for us. As we run, it's easy to put one wall of people, two walls of people, three walls and another and another between the store and us. At the same time it's like running through water, like that nightmare where your legs move but you never really seem to cover any distance.

I don't think I've ever breathed quite like this before: raspy desperate pulls for oxygen, worse—far worse—than the wind-down clock-ticking seconds of a basketball game. I'm not winded, just scared. If anyone is yelling after us, running after us, right at our heels or a mile behind, I couldn't tell you. We're cutting left and right toward the other end of the mall, and we pass each storefront like it's a moving diorama I catch out of the corner of my eye. Free Gold Hoops with Ear Piercing! Live Ringtones for Your Phone! Biggest Sale of the Season!

Just ahead I see the escalator that will take us down a level and put a bigger buffer between trouble and us. Almost there, we're almost there. I'm focusing on the escalator like it's a getaway car, like if we just make it there, then no one can catch us. We're running headlong, so much momentum built up that when we hit the top step we'll surely have to keep going, full speed forward and down, no time for apologies to anyone in our path.

That's when I hear Maddie call my name.

It can't be her, of course. There must be a hundred kids in the mall, yelling, screaming, laughing, and I know with every one of my brain cells there's no way I could hear her, no way I could pick out her voice, even if she would talk. But it doesn't matter. The rational cells are not the ones in charge right now. So when I think I hear her, I grab for Rio and we both stop cold. To anyone watching it must look like a cartoon-character stop, a couple of Wile E. Coyotes hitting one of the Roadrunner's invisible walls.

"Keep moving!" Rio tosses the words at me over his shoulder, ready to break back into a run, but I hold him still again.

"No, Rio—stop. I heard her."

"What?" His eyes say what he doesn't want to voice: You think you heard Maddie *talk*? Then you're crazy, you're panicking, at best you're just wishing too hard.

For the first time I look back behind us. No Store Manager guy. No security officer—yet. Just a bunch of Sunday afternoon shoppers detouring around us like river water parting around a rock. It looks like there's a minute to breathe, so I talk fast.

"I know it. I know it's ridiculous. But we have to stop." My voice drops. The whole time we were running, all I could think of was how much I wanted to get away, to get out of here. What I can't say out loud, what I don't even want to think in my head, is that I forgot about Maddie completely. "We have to go back and find her."

Rio lets a beat go by, giving me time. Then he catches my eye and turns on the smooth half-smile. "Fine. If you want to stop and search, no problem. Take your time. I mean, we *probably* don't have every security guard in the mall looking for us. And they *probably* don't have any big ugly guard dogs with them. And they *probably*—"

"—okay, okay." He has a point. The mall cops might still be after me, though I don't really think they have search dogs. Then it hits me, and I grab his arm. "Rio, *dogs*, that's *it!*"

"Dogs?"

"That's where she is!" I'm sure of it now.

"Don't get it."

"*Dogs!*" I give his arm a shake. "You know, in the pet store. We went right by it after we came out of the toy store. She always wants to go there."

"Yeah, it's got to be." Rio grins, knowing I'm onto something. He swings both of us around, pushing his way straight through a clump of moms and strollers. "There were puppies in the window. Fuzzy little guys. No way she could pass that up."

My mind tries to skip over the fact that if Maddie really stopped at the pet store, and we really walked on to the music store without her, it was a full fifteen minutes before I noticed she was missing. I can't deal with that thought right now so I put it on a shelf, storing it until later when I'll have time to take it down and squeeze out every last drop of guilt.

The not-noticing thing, it seems to run in the family. There's a story I tell when Mom and Dad have friends over for dinner, so I can watch the two of them squirm and blush. One night, when Rio and I were ten, we set our alarm clocks to go off at midnight and met halfway between our houses. And for the rest of the night we switched homes. Rio slept at my house, and I slept at his, and probably we both rooted around in each other's closets and drawers. In the morning I came down for breakfast in the wrong kitchen and found Mrs. Walker, Rio's mother, making pancakes. When she saw me, she pulled out my favorite strawberry syrup and had the whole plot out of me before I finished my first pancake. At my house, Rio slept late. My mom poked her head into my room and said, "Honey, time to get up." Rio says she even came in to pull up the shade and pat his shoulder, but Mom denies that part. Anyway, she didn't miss me until Mrs. Walker called her to switch us back.

So I guess it's no surprise that Mom and Dad let the first six years of Maddie's life go by without really taking in the fact that she was seriously different from other kids. Like how, at two, she was a shadow behind my mother's legs, a shadow Mom could barely peel away long enough to go to the bathroom. How, at three, Maddie liked to jabber at the rate of about a hundred words a minute—but only at home, and only to us. How they didn't have to tell Maddie not to talk to strangers; she wouldn't even talk to friends. How, at six, Maddie had a terror of starting school that was way beyond normal.

Mom was shy when she was a kid, too. She said that about a billion times, like it was a reason not to worry. Then the first-grade teacher called, wondering why Maddie wouldn't speak a single word in the classroom. That made a blip big enough to show up on my parents' radar.

Maddie has selective mutism. That's the name the doctors finally gave it. She's shy, like Mom said, but this is an ocean-deep shyness, the kind that makes her stomach tumble and her breath go short. When someone tries to talk to her—someone who isn't me or Mom or Dad—she doesn't choose silence. She just gets so scared she *can't* talk.

Right now, wherever she is, Maddie is scared. I'm betting on puppies being nearby. That's where I'll find her, and then I'll bring her home. I probably won't face too much fallout from Mom and Dad. Maddie, in her silence, is the focus of their days. While as usual I, Sadina D. Reyes, am flying more or less on my own. Just below the radar.

# Four

# MADDIE

Maddie can imagine ten different reasons it's her own fault for being left behind. She can't measure how much time has passed. If the mall closes soon, Sadina and Rio will have to leave her here as the lights die one by one and the bars slide down over the fronts of the stores. If that man who sells the animals sees her first, he'll ask questions, questions, questions, maybe even call the police to get Maddie out of the store, and there will be no Sadina to step in front of her and make it okay. No Sadina to lift her chin and say, "Forget it. You know I talk enough for both of us."

Maddie closes her eyes. In her head she can see, again, the two Dalmatian puppies that drew her in. They were white, no spots, silky and baggy-skinned. They smeared their noses against the pet-store window, and Maddie pressed her own nose onto the other side of the glass. All she wanted in that moment was to feel their softness with her fingertips. Inside, the store smelled of pee, but it didn't matter, because there were more puppies, and kittens and ferrets and rabbits, and even the fish with their feathery fins seemed to smile at her.

When Maddie feels a touch on her shoulder, she doesn't open her eyes. Better to keep her head down and her eyes shut. Maybe whoever it is will go away.

Then she hears a voice and it's saying her name. Now she has to look—and like magic Sadina is there. The real Sadina, who kisses her head again and again and hugs her hard, though they both know Maddie doesn't like that much, but just for a minute it's the right thing. Sadina pulls her to her feet, and Maddie thinks of how it feels when she lies on her arm in her sleep and it goes numb, and then in the morning the life comes back to it with a prickly tingle. Sadina says it's the blood rushing back in. Maddie's whole body feels like that now, going from numb to life, filling up with joy.

"Hey, kid, you gave us a scare. What's up with that, you like puppies better than me?" Rio teases. Maddie can't answer, can't even smile right now, though she'd like to smile to show Rio she thinks he's funny and doesn't mind his joking.

"Who wouldn't like puppies better than you?" Sadina shoots back at Rio for her, and on the way out of the store she does one more magical thing. Sadina reaches into the pen by the front window, scoops out a Dalmatian puppy, and puts it in Maddie's arms to hold for a minute. Maddie almost stops breathing, staring at the white puppy who looks back at her with round eyes, happy whether she talks or not.

# Five

# SADINA

"This is ridiculous," I say to Rio as we walk back toward the escalator.

"We got lucky," says Rio at exactly the same time.

What's ridiculous to me is that nobody has found a way to get Maddie to talk, and what's lucky is that we didn't just lose her for good. I could give Maddie the Mom-and-Dad lecture about paying attention and sticking with me, but right now isn't the time: she's walking silent but high on this happy ending, and I can't bring myself to pull her back down.

Rio keeps glancing back at her too. Between the two of us we're not going to lose her again. A lot of vigilance, a little late.

"We need a genius engineer like your mom to invent a way for Maddie to talk to us—without actually talking," Rio says. "You know, like something that reads her thoughts and says them out loud."

"Trust me, she's looked into that. It exists, sort of."

"Seriously?"

"Yeah, for people who can't move their arms or legs," I explain. "They can send brain waves to this device and it lets them control a computer screen. I think it can even move an artificial limb for them."

"Awesome. So can it talk for them?"

"My mom says nobody's tried that yet." I shrug. "Anyway, the problem is you have to be all wired up with electrodes stuck in your brain."

"Not exactly user-friendly. One thing's for sure, I wouldn't want any machine saying what I'm thinking. That could get ugly."

I laugh at the picture that puts in my head. Maddie smiles too. So she's been taking it all in. Sometimes, because she doesn't talk, I imagine she's in her own world with her thoughts, and I forget how carefully she listens.

"She needs to be able to talk to people," I say to Rio, my voice much lower now. "She needs to be able to ask for help when she needs it."

Rio doesn't answer. We're passing TecknoTurf. If I had to rate one store as our favorite, this would be it. Well, for me, maybe Playlist would take the gold—assuming Store Manager guy ever lets me back in. But TecknoTurf is the kind of store that makes you forget you have to be home for dinner, even on pizza night. It always has the latest hot thing in electronics, and whatever the next hot thing is going to be, before anyone else even knows what it is. And right now it has all of Rio's attention.

"Come on, Rio, we're not going in there. I need to get Maddie home."

Maddie knows, of course, that I want to go in as much as Rio. She gives Rio a nod and nudges me gently toward the entrance.

"You don't mind if we stop a minute? Brave girl," I say lightly, and then catch sight of Maddie's eyes. She looks at me like I'm a rock star singing a song just for her. I'm fourteen, twice her age, and I should be strong and insist on getting her home. Instead I follow Rio in, Maddie at my heels.

TecknoTurf has a whole wall of computer software. They don't stock many games, unless it's some offbeat, high-tech thing. But that's not what Rio is after, anyway. Rio and I have an idea for what could be the most amazing roller coaster ever. Rio's good at drawing on paper, but he wants this new software that helps you design things on the computer and see it all in 3D. Then you can take a virtual walk all around your design, even inside it, wherever you want to go. That's what Rio is looking for.

At least that's what I thought he was looking for. Standing at the end of the aisle, her wavy dark hair falling down her back, is Catalina. She's in a couple of my classes at school. I don't know her too well. What I do know, I don't like. But Rio picks up the pace and in the next second is by her side, tapping her shoulder and then ducking out of sight.

"Hey, Rio, I know it's you," she says, not even turning her head. Rio crowds next to her, pulling away the box she's holding.

"This is it! This is the exact software I'm looking for!"

"What a coincidence," says Catalina smoothly. She gives Rio a slow smile. So far she hasn't acknowledged that Maddie and I are here too.

"Where's the price on this thing?" Rio asks, rotating the box.

Catalina takes it back and puts in on the shelf. "Doesn't matter, it's out of your league."

I stare at Rio, waiting for his withering comeback. She's right, of course. Software like that costs more than Rio can afford. But if he's insulted, he doesn't show it. Instead he lifts his shoulders in a mild shrug.

I don't know what's gotten into him. I can't watch this. "Come on, Rio, there's supposed to be a new cell phone out. Let's see if they have it."

Catalina looks at me for the first time. She gives Maddie a little wave, jiggling the ends of her fingers like you would to a baby. Maddie looks down at the floor, her face blank.

"How old is Maddie now?" Catalina asks in a honey-sweet voice. "Like, ten or something? When is she going to learn how to talk?"

"She's seven, and she can talk fine. She just doesn't want to talk to you."

I turn and start walking back down the aisle. I'm holding my breath, and I don't let it out until I hear Rio following me. And, no surprise, Catalina trails behind.

There's only one cell phone in the display case. Typical of TecknoTurf, it's a weird one. It looks like a guy with sunglasses and surfer-boy hair. All the phone-type buttons are hidden on his back, and the voice of the person you're talking to comes out of his mouth.

"Excellent," says Rio. "But Catch-It will be better."

"What's Catch-It?" Catalina asks right away. She can never let a conversation go on too long without her.

"It's a cell phone Sadina's mom is designing."

"More than a cell phone," I add. I'm annoyed to hear a braggy edge in my own voice, like I'm working too hard to impress Catalina. I don't usually tell anyone about my mother's job—in fact I don't even think much about what she does—but for some reason my mouth goes on without my brain's okay. "It'll do things I'm not even supposed to talk about—but the best part is, the battery will last forever."

"Forever," Catalina repeats. "I doubt it."

"Well, forever like a year or two. The phone will wear out before the battery does."

Catalina tilts her head, her eyes darting back and forth between Rio and me. "If that's true," she says finally, "I'd buy one."

That's not the answer I expected. The corners of Rio's lips twitch up, and he gives me a look that says see, she has good points. Then his eyes shift over to my hand. I'm twirling a strand of hair around my finger again. A clear signal to Rio that I'm stressed, that I don't want Catalina around us. But this time he doesn't reach out to put my hair back in place. And in the next second I'm not even sure he really noticed. His attention is back on the crazy phone, and he's joking with Catalina again.

I pull my own cell phone from my pocket and call my mother to pick Maddie and me up and take us home.

# Six

# SADINA

W hen I tell Mom what happened at the mall, she closes her eyes and breathes in and out, three gulpy breaths, before she can answer.

Maddie is behind us in the back seat of the car, and Mom checks her out in the rear-view mirror. "Maddie, sweetie, are you—?"

"I'm okay!" Maddie cuts in. She's bouncing on the seat. "Mom, you know what I saw? Dalmatian puppies. And we should get one. If you saw them, you'd say yes."

As always, with just the family around her, Maddie has no trouble talking. I know what she's trying to do now by talking about the puppies. She's acting like the whole thing—getting left behind, going silent—was no big deal. She doesn't want Mom saying she can't go to the mall with me again.

When we get home, I'm relieved to see that this conversation about how I lost Maddie is going to have to be put on hold: we've got company. Flynn's red truck is in the driveway. Flynn is the engineer who's working with my mother on the new cell phone, the one with a battery that will last for years. Mom and Flynn have put in a lot of hours together at the lab so they're pretty close friends. I know Flynn, too, because he's been over for Sunday dinner a few times. He's smart and funny, the kind of guy who will wear vintage cowboy boots and wide-brim cowboy hats even though he grew up in New York City and doesn't know where milk comes from. One time Flynn had a great idea about the battery while they were talking after dinner, and he got so excited he jumped right up on the table—with his boots on—and stuck his hands up in the air like he was at the top of Mt. Everest. Now whenever he comes over, Mom makes him leave his boots at the door.

Sure enough, Flynn's boots—soft brown, with a fancy eagle design stitched on the front—are parked in the hall. Flynn and Dad are waiting for us at the dining room table, where there's a serving bowl full of chili and a loaf of bread that Flynn must have brought, because it's still warm in its paper wrapper.

Flynn smiles wide like he always does when he sees us. "Well, look who it is! Mary and Mae!"

Flynn hasn't forgotten our names—it's just a game he likes to play. He calls Maddie and me by the first names of famous women in history, and we have to guess who they are and what they're known for. It sounds a little lame but it's not, coming from Flynn.

"Mary Shelley," I guess quickly, "author of *Frankenstein*." Which I know because it was on my summer reading list for school.

"Nice try…but no." Flynn's smug face makes me think he's got a million Mary names up his sleeve so that whatever I pick will be wrong.

"Clue," I demand.

"Okay, category is famous firsts."

I think hard while Dad passes around the chili, bread, and salad, but the scientist Marie Curie is the closest I can come up with.

"Wrong again. I was thinking of Mary Walker, first woman to get a Medal of Honor," Flynn says. "I also would have accepted Mary Anderson, inventor of the first windshield wiper."

"Yeah, of course, how could I miss that?" I have to laugh as Flynn fakes a disappointed look at me.

Then he turns to Maddie. "How about you, Mae? Who are you today?"

I like the way Flynn includes Maddie in the game, though he's never gotten an answer out of her.

"I picked this one especially for you, Maddie, because I know how much you like looking at the stars."

Maddie stares down at her plate but manages a tiny headshake.

"Okay, here it is," Flynn goes on as if Maddie has given him a dozen guesses. "Mae Jemison, first African American woman in space, back in the nineties."

"I've got to wonder, Flynn, how much time you spend sitting around looking all this stuff up," my father teases.

"Some day your daughters will thank me for this, when they're inspired by *me* to be first at something." Flynn gestures toward Maddie and me with a chunk of bread, then uses it to swipe up the last of his chili. "And speaking of firsts…"

Flynn tosses the bread back into the bowl and pushes his chair away from the table. Mom winces as the chair grinds along the wood floor. Ignoring her look, Flynn darts from the room. We can hear him in the hall, digging through something. In a second he's back. He sets a small box in the middle of the table and unfolds the top flaps.

"There it is. Elizabeth and I"—he nods toward Mom—"built a prototype of Catch-It. We wanted you to be the first to see it."

 Dad, Maddie and I lean across the table, almost bumping heads as we peer into the box.

"A prototype means it's a model of what the phone is going to look like," Mom tells Maddie, and I can hear the excitement in her voice as she waits for our reaction.

I blurt out the first thing that comes into my head: "It's so small!"

"Yeah, isn't it amazing?" Flynn takes the Catch-It phone out of the box, pulls his own cell phone from his back pocket, and lines them up on the table.

Catch-It makes Flynn's phone look bulky and ridiculous. It's small enough that you could wear it on a chain around your neck, or strapped on your wrist like a watch. There's a narrow opening down one side, and when Flynn taps it, the weirdest thing happens: a screen shoots out, panels flipping open one by one until Flynn stops it with another tap. The screen is big and flexible but it doesn't collapse.

"The voice activation is just about perfect," says Mom. She takes the phone from Flynn, points it at me, and tells it, "Take a picture."

Suddenly there's me on the screen, my head tilted to the side and my nose scrunched up, permanently recorded by Catch-It.

I point to an icon with a shopping cart on it. "What's that one?"

"For buying things," Flynn explains. "Let's say you're at TecknoTurf"—Maddie and I exchange a glance—"looking around. You just point the phone at the bar code of whatever you want to buy and push the button. When you're ready to go, Catch-It charges everything to your credit card and sends all the information to the store's computers. No more checkout lines. Pretty neat, right?"

I'd love to get my hands on the phone, but Mom puts it gently back in the box.

"But the best thing is the battery, right? Won't that make you a lot of money?" I ask Flynn and Mom.

I'm sort of joking, so Flynn's response isn't what I expect. He doesn't laugh. Instead his face turns blank, like he's thinking of something deep inside his head, far away from what the rest of us can see.

"It better," he says under his breath.

Mom laughs. "I'm counting on it. Flynn, while you're here, we should go over the spec sheet…"

They head to Mom's office, taking the box with them—too bad—and leaving Dad, Maddie and me to clear the table and do the dishes. I don't mind. Dad always lets me do the dish-drying part, which is the easiest. No dealing with crusty chili bowls.

We take it easy, taking our time, and it's nice, with just the three of us working up a routine of carrying the dishes from the table to the sink, soaping them up and rinsing them clean, rubbing them dry with a blue-striped terry-cloth towel, then sending them on home to their cabinets and shelves. Dad starts pretending he's a malfunctioning robot, putting everything away in the wrong place, and Maddie follows along behind him, setting things right and laughing like crazy.

It's almost an hour later when I take one last trip into the dining room to put away the placemats. Flynn's phone is still on the table. I scoop it up and take it down to Mom's office. But when I look in, she's the only one there.

"Where's Flynn?"

Mom looks up, her attention still half on the papers in front of her. "He left a while ago. Just looked at his watch, said he had to go, and rushed out." She shakes her head, amused. "That's Flynn."

"Well, he left this." I hold up the phone.

"Oh, he'll be missing that. Would you call his house and tell him it's here?"

"Sure." I call him from the phone in the kitchen so I don't disturb Mom any more. I'm expecting his voicemail so when Flynn actually answers I'm not ready, and he jumps in ahead of me.

"Hey, Sadina, I think I forgot my phone. Have you seen it?"

"That's why I was calling. It was on the table."

"Do me a favor and make sure it's off?"

I can't pass up the chance to tease him. "Well, if someone would just invent a new battery that lasts more than a few hours, you wouldn't have to worry about it, would you?"

"Seriously, Sadina, please just turn it off. I don't want to bother anyone if it rings."

Okay, does that make any sense? We've all heard his so-NOT-cool Star Wars ring tone before. Whatever. I can still be polite. "It's off. Do you want my mom to bring it to work tomorrow?"

"I might not be in the lab, so I'll stop by and get it. Thanks, Sadina. I really appreciate it. Excellent. Thanks again."

Weird: that was kind of over-the-top gratitude for making sure his phone was in off mode. Weirder: he actually called me by my real name—not Hilary or Anne or Aida.

Weirdest: None of this is even truly weird, because it's Flynn. Anyway, I'm tired and I don't care. I've had enough to think about today. I head to bed, and I'm pretty sure there's nothing that could keep me awake for another minute.

# Seven

# SADINA

That night I'm kept awake by the soft sound of voices. They start in the room below mine. Not long after I switch off the light and curl into bed, the voices reach my room, filling it up like smoke. One voice is pitched low, the other higher, a humming and rolling duet. They should ease me into sleep. Instead my mind—my whole body—keeps straining to turn the sounds into words I can understand.

I try pulling a blanket up over my head. It's dark and pleasant under here but, guess what, no quieter. Sound waves, it turns out, can travel pretty easily through fifty percent cotton, fifty percent polyester.

The voices belong to my parents. For hours they've been pitching words back and forth in a conversation I would love to hear. I'm sure I know the title of their talk: What Do We Do About Maddie? It's clear she's not getting any better, especially after my mess-up of losing her at the mall today.

Maddie's room is down the hall, so maybe she can't hear the voices. I hope not. Sometimes Maddie makes me think of that fairy tale about the princess and the pea. The one where the poor country girl comes to a castle and sleeps on a big pile of mattresses and then wakes up all achy and unhappy because there was a pea at the bottom of the pile. And the prince believes she must be a princess, because only a princess could be that sensitive. Or, in my opinion, that thin-skinned. Anyway, Maddie's like that. She can't stand the tags on her T-shirts and she hates wearing socks. She holds her hands over her ears when the vacuum is running or when Rio laughs too loudly. When my friends come over Dad is always telling us to quiet down.

It's funny that Dad is the one who works the hardest to make Maddie's world quiet and cushioned. He grew up in the middle of Springfield, population 150,000, and the noise is one of the things he still misses. He says there are nights he can't go to sleep without it, and that's when he'll put on his earphones and crank the volume on his music player, trying to recreate the clatter and blare of traffic that went right under his bedroom window when he was a kid.

We moved out of the thick of the city when I was three but we're still a long way from countryside and crickets. Here the houses are skinny and three stories high because there's just no room to spread out. Each home stands straight over its own little piece of earth, trying not to nudge shoulders with its neighbors. Mostly it's a pretty quiet neighborhood, though some summer nights Dad has to close Maddie's windows and pull down the shades to muffle the sound of Mrs. Turner, the nurse, coming off her midnight shift and grinding into a tight parking spot, and Calloway, the dog at the end of the block, barking out a steady beat.

But right now it's Dad and Mom making a buzz. And if their voices are reaching Maddie's room then, like me, she's not sleeping.

It's no use. There's no point staying in bed. If I can just hear what they're talking about, see where this conversation is heading, then maybe I won't have to spend what's left of the night in my blanket cave. But I can't let them know I'm listening. When it comes to Maddie, I don't always get straight answers. If I ask them outright they'll probably shut down and tell me everything is fine.

Some people are skilled at being stealthy. Catalina, just for an example. She's always showing up where she's not wanted, so I bet she's good at covert operations. I bet she could slide out of bed and make it to the door and not step on a single floorboard that creaks. I bet she could get down the stairs silent as a snake. Anyway, the point is, some people are naturals at this, and I'm not one of them.

As I get out of bed, the book I was reading tips over the side of the mattress and clunks onto the floor. I freeze. But the voices below keep going. I cross my room up on my toes, as if that would make me lighter. When I reach my door and open it, the hall ahead is mineshaft black. It's past midnight now, so the timer that controls the hallway light has clicked to off. I can't imagine navigating sightless down that tunnel. I inch back to my nightstand to find a flashlight. The drawer sticks and then gives with a whiny creak. I have to fumble through tissue packs, wristbands, a mini-book on dreams, some Pokémon cards I collected when I was ten, and about five tubes of lip balm before I find the flashlight. None of this is silent or even the tiniest bit stealthy. I freeze again and hold my breath to hear better. The voices roll on. Can't they hear me? What do they think is going on up here? Oh, it's just Sadina, straightening up her room in the middle of the night?

The flashlight battery is dead. Now there's nothing I can do but press my hand to the wall and fumble down the hallway by feel.

Walking around a house at night is like crossing past a No Trespassing sign. You don't belong. During the hours of darkness the house belongs to the refrigerator humming from its corner, to the photographs staring from the mantelpiece, to the clocks marking off the minutes before the people take over again. I'm invading their territory and I can't even see where I'm going. It is so, *so* dark.

The way I discover I've reached the top of the staircase is that when I step forward, the floor is gone.

My foot lands hard on the top stair, and I stumble and pitch down five more steps before I finally catch the handrail. I sit there, breathless, rubbing an elbow that feels like it somehow connected with solid rock on the way down. The voices have finally gone quiet. There are footsteps, and someone flips a switch in the front hall. The light spills around the corner and makes it partway up the stairwell. I can see where I'm going now, but if anyone heads for the stairs, my cover is gone.

"What was it?" It's my mother's voice.

"Came from outside, I think," my father says. I hear him open the front door and step onto the porch. "I can't see anything."

"Dogs in the garbage again?"

"Doesn't look like it. Hey, where's the recycle bin? Wasn't it Sadina's turn to put it out?"

Oh shoot, I forgot to take out the recycle bin before I went to bed. Trust Dad to spot that, even when he's supposed to be investigating a mysterious thump in the night. There's no answer from Mom, so probably she's just shrugging and shaking her head in disappointment at my lack of responsibility. Footsteps again, a door shuts, and the voices start again, but lower now. They've already forgotten the noise. Well, that's a lucky break, I guess. But there's a part of me that wants to jump off the stairs, yelling as loudly as I can. What does it take to get noticed around here?

Maybe it's time to stop the stealthy approach. Maybe I should just knock on the door and ask them what's going on. The problem is, I don't think they'll tell me. They don't want me to worry, not getting that what you *don't* know can be scarier than what you do know. And the truth is, I'm scared for Maddie.

Not talking isn't so bad when you're a little kid. It hasn't kept Maddie from making friends: seven-year-olds, after all, aren't too hard on each other. But what happens next? Is she going to get better, start talking to people other than Mom and Dad and me? Or will she turn into the girl everyone stares at and laughs at because she can't speak for herself? The one girl who doesn't get asked to the ninth-grade dance, and who couldn't answer yes even if she was asked? I don't want to let her get there. I want to help Maddie talk.

And, at least, I know what I can do to start. I get up from the stairs and walk firmly down the hall—perfectly quiet now that I'm no longer trying. I lean against my mother's office door and press my ear tightly against it.

Time to collect some information.

# Eight

# SADINA

Eavesdropping is actually not that easy, especially if you haven't thought ahead and planted any cool, micro-sized, voice-amplifying transmitter gadgets around the room, like they do in the movies. I can tell my mother's voice apart from my father's now, but they're talking more quietly than before, and all I can pick up are words and phrases, not quite enough to piece together the whole conversation.

Mom: "…right in front of me…the whole time…"

Dad: "…won't stop…"

Mom: "…don't know how to tell…"

Long pause. Sounds of scraping, like a chair being dragged along the floor.

Dad: "…make sure we know…the consequences…"

Mom: "…don't tell her yet…"

Whoa, red flag. What's that all about? Consequences? That sounds bad. And what don't they want to tell me yet? My stomach gives a sick little lurch, because their words add up to one thing, and I know exactly what it is.

They're talking about sending Maddie away.

Here's how I know: A family down the street has a little boy who's deaf, and when he was six they sent him to a special school so he could learn sign language. He stays there full time. I think he's only home on holidays and in the summer. Ever since I heard about that little boy, I've been thinking there's probably a special school like that for kids with selective mutism. For kids like Maddie. But Mom and Dad don't know how Maddie would handle it, what the consequences would be. And they don't want to tell me yet because they know how much I would hate the idea.

Maddie, at a school where everyone is a stranger. Maddie, surrounded by people trying to make her talk all the time. Maddie, forced to wear a uniform with scratchy socks. Those are the images running through my head. They make me feel weak, like my knees are going to buckle beneath me.

I've got to stop this. Without giving myself time to think, I open the office door and walk straight into the middle of the room.

What happens next is like someone setting off a pile of firecrackers: everything starts to pop.

Mom and Dad both jump, staring at me with wide eyes.

"Sadina!" Dad shouts. "What are you doing down here?"

Mom has something in her hand and, without taking her eyes off me, she jams it into the top drawer of her desk and slams the drawer shut.

I square my shoulders. "You *can't* send Maddie away!" The words were supposed to come out loud and angry, but my voice sounds high and thin.

Mom and Dad stare some more, like I'm someone they've never seen before.

"Send Maddie away?" Dad says. "What are you talking about?"

"I heard what you said. You think Maddie's never going to learn to talk. But you *can't* send her away." My voice is getting stronger. "I can't believe you're even thinking about this."

"I don't know what you thought you heard," Dad says, "but we're not sending Maddie anywhere."

"More to the point, why do you even think that?" Mom asks. Her eyes narrow. "Were you listening at the door?"

I can't believe it. This is not how the conversation is supposed to be going. "We're talking about Maddie's *life*, Mom. This is about her whole future. What's best for *her*. Who cares if I was listening at the door?"

Mom cares, apparently. A lot. Her lips are pressed together, which happens when she's angry but doesn't want to let it out.

"Sadina, I asked you, were you listening at the door?"

"Okay, yes. Sort of. I mean, I came down the stairs and I could hear voices and I followed the sound to your office. I couldn't sleep." For the second time in twenty-four hours, I get the feeling I'm not making sense.

"That conversation was between your father and me," Mom says, her voice tight. "It has nothing to do with you, and you had no right to listen in."

"What else am I supposed to do? You never tell me anything." That's it, that's exactly how I feel: like I'm trying to read a book but a bunch of pages are missing.

"You need to get back to your room," Mom says, letting each word snap out of her mouth.

I can tell she means it. I was fired up for a fight to keep Maddie home and safe, and now all I'm doing is defending my right to eavesdrop. Maybe my room is the best place to be. I want to argue for Maddie's sake, but I need time to sort all this out.

Without another word, I turn away. Dad follows me out of the office.

"Sadina," he says gently as I start up the stairs.

I turn back to him, hoping I'm about to be thrown some scrap of information or comfort.

But Dad gestures toward the kitchen. "Forget something?" The blue recycle bin is still sitting next to the sink. Mom and Dad recycle everything they can. And they won't buy anything that has too much packaging. Mom always says she doesn't want to leave too big a footprint on the earth. Which means I get the job of putting the bin out for the recycle truck every Sunday night.

"Right," I say. "I'll take care of it now."

When Dad is out of sight, I carry the bin to the front porch, dump every last bottle and can straight into the garbage can, and get to bed.

Twenty minutes later, I'm still wide awake. Back to the porch again, where I pull the bottles and cans out of the garbage and return them one by one to the recycle bin.

Now my conscience is clear, but it doesn't help. I still can't sleep.

# Nine

# MADDIE

"It's 12:58 am. Why aren't you sleeping?"

The message blinks red from the clock above Maddie's bed. The clock was a birthday present from Sadina, who bought it at TecknoTurf. Maddie loves watching the clock flash out a new message. Sadina and Rio wrote them all and programmed them into the clock. Maddie's favorite so far is the one that shows up at bedtime: "Maddie Reyes, it's half past nine, can you get to bed on time?"

But Maddie never really gets ready for bed that early. Dad calls Maddie a night owl. She loves the sound of that. Maddie looks out her bedroom window at the black sky and the banana-shaped moon and imagines herself perched on a tree limb, feathery and alert. She has heard that owls can turn their heads almost all the way around, and that's what she would do, so no one could sneak up on her. Her owl voice would be smooth and pretty as a song, hoo-hoo-hoo-ing all through the night.

Maddie checks the clock in time to see the message change again. "It's 1:00 am. Pat your cat and GET TO BED NOW!"

Maddie laughs out loud and scoops Bella the cat up from the floor. Bella, Maddie knows, is not very pat-able. Instead of fur and whiskers she has shiny metal skin and sensors behind her blue plastic eyes. Bella is a robotic cat. She can purr when you scratch behind her ears and hiss when you touch her paws. She can even do tricks, like roll over, though sometimes she gets stuck on her back halfway through the roll. Most of all, Bella is good to talk to. She knows Maddie's voice. When Maddie talks—only Maddie, no one else—Bella tips her head to the side and meows.

And now there is a new thing Bella can do. Maddie has just figured it out, and it's such a big and amazing new thing that she has to tell Sadina right away. She knows Sadina is awake too. She's heard her sister going up and down the hall, heard the angry voices from downstairs. She should let Sadina sleep, but morning is too far away.

With Bella tucked under her arm, Maddie pushes open Sadina's door just enough to see her sister in bed.

That's good; Sadina looks happy to see her.

"What's the matter, Princess?" Sadina is smiling. "Is there a pea under your mattress?"

Maddie sticks out her tongue. She knows that story too.

Sadina is lying on top of her quilt, the puffy one with pink and yellow stripes. Sadina always says she hates it, along with the pictures of kittens and posters of forgotten bands on her wall. Every morning at breakfast she says to Mom that these things all belong to a little girl's room and they all have to go. That sounds like a good idea to Maddie. She'd like the pictures and posters for herself.

Maddie sits on the edge of Sadina's bed with Bella between them.

"Bella has a big surprise for you," Maddie tells her.

"Yeah, what's that? Is she finally using her litter box?" Sadina teases.

"Noooo, Sadina. Stop it. This is a real surprise." Maddie pauses, letting the moment build. "Bella can *think*!"

Sadina stares. "What do you mean, she can think?"

"You know how you can tell her to sit and lie down and dance and all that, 'cause it's in her program?" Maddie asks.

Sadina nods.

"Well now Bella's doing new things all by herself. Like I said it was time for bed, and after I was in bed I looked at her and she was in her bed too, and her eyes were closed. And I never even said the words *Lie Down* like you're supposed to." Maddie is so excited she feels like a shaken-up soda bottle, with words bubbling right out of her lips. "And then I had a bunch of books on the floor and I asked her which one I should read. She walked over to *Harriet the Spy* and stood on top of it. That's my favorite one! And I never even taught her what a book is!"

The look on Sadina's face is funny, like she doesn't know what to say.

"It's really true!" Maddie picks Bella up and looks into her eyes. "I talk to her all the time and now she can really understand me. Even better than a real cat."

"I don't know, Maddie. I mean, she's a robot, right? She can't really think. But I guess maybe she could learn new words."

Maddie isn't sure what she expected Sadina to do with this big news. Yell for Mom and Dad. Grab Maddie and dance. Talk about what else they can teach Bella now that she can think. Not this. This is Sadina not believing, and now Maddie doesn't know what to say or do.

"Maddie. Look at me. You don't really think she's real, do you?"

Maddie feels her face turn hot. She *does* think it.

"You don't know everything! Bella understands me!" Maddie shouts it out, as loudly as she can. All Sadina cares about are her stupid music and her stupid room. She doesn't even care that Bella is no ordinary robotic cat.

All of Maddie's excitement has sunk right back into her stomach, weighing it down. She can't stay here another second. She turns her back on Sadina and darts from the room, slamming the door behind her with all the strength she has. That's one loud sound she wouldn't mind making again.

# SADINA

An hour ago I thought this day couldn't get any worse. I lost my sister, failed completely as a covert agent, and got my parents mad. But now I can add to the list: I've let Maddie down. Could I have made a bigger mess of everything?

I need to pour this whole crazy day out of my head into someone else's ears. Rio, of course. He'll always listen.

I tap my computer out of its sleep mode and see that Rio is online.

**lady_sadie:** (that's my screen name): u there?
**redriver494:** *(that's Rio): yeah whats up?*
**lady_sadie:** worst day EVER
**redriver494:** *y*
**lady_sadie:** Maddie is scaring me
**redriver494:** *is she ok?*
**lady_sadie:** she's talking to her cat
**redriver494:** *so what? she does that all the time*
**lady_sadie:** she just told me she thinks it's real

There's no answer, like Rio's reading that line over a few times. Then…

**redriver494:** *????*
**lady_sadie:** she said it can think—it does stuff that's not in its program

| | |
|---|---|
| redriver494: | *the robot cat?* |
| lady_sadie: | yeah, the robot cat—she said it understands when she talks to it |
| redriver494: | *maybe shes just pretending* |
| lady_sadie: | no she means it…she got so mad when I didn't believe her |

So mad—that's an understatement. Now that I've written it down, I can see Maddie again, *I-hate-you-how-could-you-not-believe-me* written all over her face in razor-sharp high resolution. There's no question: she really believed it.

| | |
|---|---|
| lady_sadie: | do u think there's any way? |
| redriver494: | *meaning?* |
| lady_sadie: | any way Bella can really think? |
| redriver494: | *yeah right robots can think and so can computers…thats y mine crashes right before I save stuff—then it laughs at me* |
| lady_sadie: | not funny |
| redriver494: | *sry—r u serious about this?* |
| lady_sadie: | YES!!! what do u think, could anyone ever make a robot that thinks for itself? |
| redriver494: | *idk I guess maybe, but you would need some mad programming skills* |
| lady_sadie: | you'd have to program it to think like people do |
| redriver494: | *yeah awesome, as long as it doesn't think like YOU* |
| lady_sadie: | ur not as funny as u think |
| redriver494: | *maybe this isnt even me, maybe i programmed my computer to talk to u so i can go catch some zzzs—how would u know* |
| lady_sadie: | thats easy i just ask you a question a computer can't answer |
| redriver494: | *so go ahead* |

There's a part of me that knows Rio is trying to distract me, giving me a challenge to pull me out of the world of Maddie and everything else. That's okay. It's working.

| | |
|---|---|
| lady_sadie: | listen up, rio-bot, I got it: whats the top selling CD right now |
| redriver494: | *that the best u can do? totally no good…i could program any computer to answer that* |
| lady_sadie: | fine |
| lady_sadie: | how about this one |
| lady_sadie: | I'm not really asking |
| lady_sadie: | it's just a test to see if ur real |
| redriver494: | *ok so say it already* |
| lady_sadie: | do you like catalina? |
| redriver494: | *strike two, way too easy, computer could say yes or no and either way it doesnt prove anything* |
| lady_sadie: | u just don't want to answer, but ok one more try: tell me all the ways I'm different from catalina |

A full minute goes by. If I thought he really couldn't come up with an answer I'd be mad. But I know his mind is just churning away trying to figure out if a computer could handle that one like a person could.

| | |
|---|---|
| redriver494: | *might work* |

Coming from Rio, that means it was a pretty good question.

| | |
|---|---|
| redriver494: | *got 2 go, mom yelling* |
| lady_sadie: | ok cya |

Sign off, shut down, get to bed. Rio took my mind off Maddie for a little while. But I still don't believe that Bella the robotic cat can think.

# Eleven

# MADDIE

**M**addie stands at the corner a block away from her house, waiting for the school bus. She stares straight down, so that all she can see are the tops of her brown boots and a circle of sidewalk. The wind brushes red and yellow leaves into sight, then out again, their dry, curled edges scratching the concrete. One leaf catches against the edge of Maddie's boot. She shakes her foot, setting the leaf free to catch up with the others.

There are five kids at the bus stop, loud with Monday morning chatter. Sadina is there too, because they take the same bus. But Maddie doesn't want to see or listen to Sadina or anyone else today. There are too many other things to think about.

When Maddie woke up this morning, Bella was standing beside her bed. After Maddie ate her cereal and got dressed, she stood in the doorway of her room, staring into Bella's shiny blue

eyes. Bella wanted to come to school, Maddie was sure. But there's a school rule about that: don't bring anything other than your backpack and lunch box and homework.

At seven thirty Mom yelled from downstairs: "Hurry, Maddie, you have to go *now*! And don't forget your jacket if you want to go outside at recess."

Maddie couldn't move. She felt like the dog walker she saw at the park, holding tight to two leashes that pulled in two different directions at once. In the end she couldn't leave Bella behind. Maddie put the cat in her backpack, zipped it shut, and hoped no one would notice it was twice as fat and twice as heavy as ever before.

Now, at the bus stop, Maddie crouches down and slides the backpack off her shoulder. She'll check on Bella without anyone seeing, to let her know everything's okay and there's really nothing scary about going on a bus. Without looking up, Maddie pulls the zipper back inch by inch until she sees the rounded top of Bella's head.

There's a shuffling sound beside her. Maddie keeps her head down but the red boots that belong to Laurel's feet just come closer. Laurel is in Maddie's class and hangs out with other girls, the noisy ones who never really pay attention to Maddie.

"What's that?" says Laurel.

Maddie starts to slide the zipper back the other way. It's too late. Laurel sticks out her hand, fast, and pulls the backpack wide open.

"What is it?" she asks again. "A cat?"

Maddie knows Laurel isn't trying to be mean, but her voice is loud, and the other girls at the bus stop drift toward them.

"It's a robotic cat," says Laurel's friend Stephanie. "My cousin has one of those. It walks and meows and stuff like that."

"It can say meow?" Another voice. Maddie still hasn't looked up, but she can tell it belongs to Emerson, a fourth-grader. "Maddie can't even say meow!"

All around Maddie's head there is laughter.

"Maddie, you're dumber than a robot!"

"You're dumber than a *cat!*"

She holds very still. The girls' voices rise higher and Maddie pretends she can't hear what they're saying now.

"Bus!" It's Sadina. With one word she sweeps them away. The girls leave Maddie and crowd at the curb, watching the flat yellow front of the bus glide toward them like a ship coming in from the sea. Maddie waits until the smell of diesel fills her nose, until the doors swing out with a crank and a whoosh, until the last boot disappears up the grooved steps.

"Let's go," says Sadina. Her voice is not soft and coaxing like it usually is. It doesn't matter. Maddie has Bella today, and that's all the strength she needs to sling the pack onto her shoulder, rise up tall, and climb into the waiting bus.

# Twelve

# SADINA

**M**addie takes a seat three places ahead of me on the bus and won't look back. All I can see is a cap of curly brown hair rising above the edge of the seat. Well, that's fine. A little space between us is probably a good idea right now.

I can't believe she's bringing that cat to school. All morning I've put up "Do Not Cross this Line" signs in my brain, to keep out thoughts of what I said to Maddie last night. I don't want to think about it. I know I let her down. But what was I supposed to do, play along and pretend Bella is real?

When I saw Laurel and her little pack circling around Maddie at the bus stop, I should have stopped them right away. I waited a minute too long. I could say it's because I want her to learn to stand up for herself. The truth is I was just tired, really really tired of standing between Maddie and the world. Mom sometimes calls me Maddie's guardian angel. Rio thinks that image is all wrong: he says I'm Maddie's enforcer. That's what those hockey guys are called, the ones who get in fights for the rest of the team. I've seen pictures of them, and even though I don't have any black eyes or missing teeth I know exactly how they feel.

Rio gets on the bus at the next stop. Usually he doesn't sit with me, because then his friends start with the boyfriend-girlfriend jokes. But today I catch his eye and pat the seat, and with a shrug Rio slides in next to me, his backpack bumping my feet. He smells like Sword aftershave, and his black hair is shiny with something he's brushed into it.

"What's up, dude?" Rio says, punching my shoulder lightly.

I roll my eyes.

I watch Rio's face morph from smile to serious as he gets that I need to talk. "That thing you said about Maddie last night was weird," he says, quiet enough so that she won't hear. "She thinks her cat is real?"

"She says it understands her. Which is weird enough. But there's something else."

Rio gives a quick nod. "Thought so. You were really freaked out. What's going on?"

"It's my mom and dad. It was late, like midnight, and I could hear them talking in Mom's office. So I went down and just walked in on them." There, that's a neat little summary of my miserable attempt at 007 spy maneuvers.

I hang onto my seat as the bus almost misses a stop. The Reed twins get on and take the front seat. That means we're about half a mile away and two more stops from school.

"They thought I heard what they were talking about, and Mom got so mad," I go on.

"So what *were* they talking about? Maddie?"

"I'm pretty sure." I start to say more, to tell him my theory that they're going to send her away. But it's funny, now that I'm not tired and tripped up in the dark, how I'm really not so sure anymore. So I skip over that. "Right when I walked in, Mom had something in her hand. She stuck it in a drawer like she didn't want me to see it."

Rio jumps on that. "What was it?"

"I told you, she put it away in the drawer."

"And you didn't go back later and check it out?"

"Rio, come on. I can't just walk in there and start going through her desk."

"So what do you think it is?"

"Something to do with Maddie, I guess. Something's got to be going on, and if Mom doesn't want to tell me about it, it must be bad news."

"Ergo," Rio says, showing off his spattering of Latin, "you've got to find out what it is."

"She probably locked the drawer, though."

"That doesn't have to stop you." Rio looks at me sideways. "I know a few tricks."

Rio the lock picker. Sure. He's got to be kidding me. Right?

Here's the vision that comes into my head. Rio and I, dark as moon shadows, glide into my mother's office. We're so quiet it's like someone has pressed a mute button. We reach her desk, look at each other, and exchange a wordless message that this is it, now or never. Rio pulls something from the pocket of his sweatshirt that glints silver and looks like a tool from a dentist's tray. He slides it into the keyhole of the top drawer and a second later turns to me, triumphant. The drawer is open. I push past Rio to look inside and see…

Never mind. The whole thing is ridiculous. That's not my style. Whatever is locked in that drawer, I'm not meant to see it. It may not have anything to do with Maddie anyway. And if it does, I guess Mom has the right to withhold information she doesn't want me to see. I guess it's the adults who should make the decisions. It's not like my opinion counts anyway.

But…I'd like to judge for myself whether I can handle whatever's going on. And that would be easier to do if I could just see what's in that drawer.

Now I feel like I'm stuck in a traffic circle. Round and round, without enough logic to reason my way to the off ramp.

At least I can get off this bus. We've made it to school, and Rio is already halfway down the aisle to the door. He turns back and points a finger at me.

"Midnight," he says. "Meet where we always do. It's the only way."

He's out of the bus before I can even laugh. Paulie, one of the Reed twins, shoulders his way into the aisle ahead of me.

"Midnight," says Paulie, his voice dipped as low as he can make it. "It's the only way, girl. You and me, we'll leave this town and never come back."

It's the worst cowboy imitation I've ever heard, but Rick, the other Reed twin, loves it. They follow me all the way into homeroom, pointing their fingers at me like guns and trading lines.

"Midnight, Sadie."

"It's the only way."

"Meet where we always do."

"Yeah, that's right, girl. Midnight."

I ignore them—it's the only way to deal with Paulie and Rick—but they don't quit. It's weird: The more they say it, the more it starts to sound like a plan.

# Thirteen

# SADINA

"That," says Catalina, "is the stupidest plan I've ever heard."

We're in Mrs. Weber's English Lit class, talking about Romeo and Juliet—one of Shakespeare's most beautiful plays, gushes Mrs. Weber, and the most famous love story ever. But Catalina doesn't think much of it.

We just read the part where Juliet drinks a potion that makes her look dead, so she can get away from her family to be with Romeo. If you don't know the story, here's what happens next: Romeo finds Juliet, thinks she's really dead, and kills himself. Juliet wakes up, sees Romeo dead, and kills herself. So Catalina has a point. If they were shooting for happily ever after, this plan didn't really get it done.

Back on the first day of class, Mrs. Weber said she wanted our honest opinions about whatever we're reading. You don't have to love Shakespeare to get an A. But if you don't like something, you have to be ready to back it up. "Surprise me." That's Mrs. Weber's favorite expression. "Tell me something I haven't heard before. And give me a reason to believe you."

Catalina's comment doesn't pass that test. Mrs. Weber smiles like she's heard it a thousand times.

"Okay, let's step back for a minute," she says. "Let's think about what Romeo and Juliet were up against." She turns to the blackboard and picks up her chalk, a can't-miss-it neon-bright lime green. "What forces in society were keeping Romeo and Juliet from getting together?"

Monica, who likes to sit up front so she doesn't have to wear her glasses, slowly raises a hand. "Well, obviously, their parents hated each other."

"Good. The feud between the Montagues and Capulets," says Mrs. Weber, writing FAMILY HISTORY in big letters on the board. She twirls the chalk in her fingers. By the end of class her hands are always covered in lime green dust. "Anything else?"

We're all quiet. No one wants to get it wrong. In other classes, the teachers might end up feeding us the answers. But that won't happen here. Mrs. Weber lets the silence stretch.

"Didn't Juliet's father want her to marry another guy?" Paulie finally offers. I can't really warm up to Paulie, he's just too annoying, but I have to say he's smart. He can pull meaning out of passages of poetry that are so obscure you feel like you're reading in the dark.

Mrs. Weber gives a little nod. "Absolutely. Juliet's father chose a husband for her. That's how their society worked. And Juliet was supposed to honor that arrangement."

The chalk goes back into action, this time printing out SOCIETY'S EXPECTATIONS. I like how she takes our fumbling words, mixes them in her hands, and turns them into a row of block letters that look confident and clever.

"So here are Romeo and Juliet, a boy and a girl your age, who have to make a very big decision." Mrs. Weber's arms sweep out, a visual demonstration of *big*. "Are they going to be loyal to their families and their society? Or should they be loyal to their own feelings, which say they belong together?"

Her voice drops. "As you know, Romeo and Juliet choose to follow their hearts."

Paulie and about half the class fill the room with snorts of laughter and fake mushy kissing sounds.

"There's no way I'd ruin my life over some guy," adds Catalina. She reaches up to tuck a strand of hair behind her ear but can't hide a quick glance at Jerome, her last boyfriend.

"Not a lot of believers in true love, I see," says Mrs. Weber. "Well, here's what I want you think about."

Those are the words she always uses to wrap things up and give us our homework assignment. We all reach for our pencils.

"Considering the forces Romeo and Juliet were up against, was this ending inevitable? Or were there some points where they could have acted differently or made other choices to bring things down a different path?" She pauses as the end-of-class bell lets out a shrill bleat. "One-page essay, due Wednesday, and remember I like to see direct quotes from the book to support your ideas."

I scribble the words in my class planner, while around me chairs scrape, backpacks zip and thump, voices pulse right into maximum volume. I'm usually among the first ones out the door—not that I don't like this class, but next period is lunch and sometimes it takes twenty minutes just to get through the line. Today I take my time.

That essay question about choosing a different path has snagged in my brain. It feels like when a comb catches in a matted bit of hair, stopping you short until you straighten it out.

I rewind the past twenty-four hours in my mind, play it back fast. This much I can see: I've already made a couple of choices when it comes to dealing with Maddie. One, that I won't let her slide silently through her days. I want her to be able to talk. Two, that I'll listen at doors if that's what it takes to find out what Mom and Dad are planning for her. What I'm not so sure about is where this path is heading. I've never thought of this before, that something I do or say today might be like choosing a train at the station. It might be one that runs east instead of west, so that much later when it reaches its destination I might step off and suddenly realize it's not at all where I wanted to be.

It turns out the middle of a classroom is not a great place to stand if you need a little quiet time to think things over.

Catalina pokes me in the back.

"Move along, Reyes, you're blocking the aisle," she says. "I have places to go, even if your life has no purpose besides hanging out here."

I'm not really in the mood for matching wits with Catalina right now, but I have to answer, just like my knee has to kick when it gets tapped with a rubber hammer at the doctor's office. I open my mouth as she shoves by, but snap it back shut before a coherent word can come out. There's a voice coming over the intercom, and I'm pretty sure it said Rio's name. Sure enough, after a brief interlude of static, I hear it again.

"Rio Walker, please report to Mrs. Mercer's office now." That's the principal's office. And that's never good.

Rio's not in the classroom any more, but he must be right outside the door in the hall, because I can hear some guys hooting and razzing him. Even without seeing him I know Rio's face is probably turning red. He doesn't much like being the center of attention.

"Wherefore art thou Rio? Deny thy name and refuse to go!" Paulie yells in a painful misquote of Romeo. Good thing Shakespeare wasn't around to hear that.

By the time I reach the door, Rio is out of sight. In all the time I've known him, he's been called to the principal's office only once before. Last year, in eighth grade, he got caught up on the fringes of a food fight in the cafeteria. The lunch monitor said she saw Rio with an apple in his hand. That part was true. But Rio said he wasn't planning on throwing it. He just meant to keep it away from his friend Scott, a first-string pitcher with a strong arm and perfect aim. I've been friends with Rio long enough to know that he's no good at lying. I believed him. No one else did.

At this point it doesn't matter if I have time for lunch or not. With Rio added to the list of things I'm worried about, I don't think I could get through a plate of nachos anyway.

# Fourteen

# SADINA

The next time I see Rio, his hands are rounded into fists and he doesn't even know it. He's that mad.

School is out and we're on the bus headed for home. I lean over the back of my seat, listening to Rio reconstruct the scene with Mrs. Mercer, the principal.

"I got to Mrs. Mercer's office and she was in there with Mr. J," Rio says.

Mr. J—that's Mr. Jaworski. I'm in his math class, and Rio is in his computer-aided design class.

"I thought I knew what was happening," Rio goes on. "I thought Mr. J must have told her about my design project and Mrs. Mercer thought it was so cool I should get an award." Rio's not bragging. His design is good. It's a wheelchair ramp for this house belonging to a guy who got hurt and can't walk up and down the stairs anymore.

"So I had this big stupid grin on my face when Mrs.

Mercer started talking. She asked me about that new design software Mr. J bought for the class and if I'd used it yet and stuff like that. It was probably like five minutes before I figured out what was going on."

"I don't get it," says Scott from the seat behind Rio's. "What was going on?"

"They think I stole it," Rio says flatly.

"Stole what?"

"The software." Rio keeps his face carefully blank but it's all in his eyes. This is eating him up. "It's been missing since Friday. They said I was the last one in the classroom."

"Mr. *Jaworski* said you stole it?" I ask. This isn't making sense. I've only known Mr. J for a couple of months—since school started—but he doesn't seem like the kind of teacher who would turn a guy in without asking a few questions first.

"No. I think he believes me," says Rio. "But, remember, he wasn't even there Friday. We had a substitute, and she says I stayed in the classroom when she went to lunch. Which I did, but I was just going to load the software and surprise Mr. J." Rio draws a deep breath. "So I guess it looks pretty bad."

"That stinks," says Scott.

"Totally," says Monica. I didn't even know she was listening, but now she half rises from her seat two rows back to give Rio a sympathetic nod. "What happens now? Did you get suspended?"

"No," Rio tells her. "And since my record is clean and Mr. J vouches for me, Mrs. Mercer said she's not taking any action yet. But she's going to call my parents and she said it'd be better for me if I tell the truth. Which means she's already made up her mind I'm guilty."

I wish there were a disconnect button between thought and action, because what happens next is bad. The thought that appears in the back of my brain suddenly pops right out of my mouth. "Isn't that the same software you wanted to buy at the mall?"

There's a dead little silence from Rio. Then he says slowly, "What do you mean?"

"Nothing. Rio, I didn't mean anything." I'm backpedaling as fast as I can. But the awful part is, I did, sort of. He was looking at that exact software at TecknoTurf. I know how much he wants it. But how could I even think that? I'm Rio's best friend. I flash back to Rio with me at the mall, stepping up to face that store manager who thought I was stealing a CD. That's what "best friends" looks like.

"Rio, seriously, I believe you," I say quickly, but even I can hear how unconvincing it sounds. This is crazy. Of course Rio couldn't have stolen the software. I should have thought that right away, should have been way ahead of Scott and Monica to tell him so.

"I know," Rio says. "It's okay."

But when the bus reaches his stop, he gets off without looking me in the eye. No "see you, Sadina." No "call me later."

I twist around in my seat to watch him through the window. He stands on the sidewalk without moving, facing the driveway up to his house. His shoulders are hunched forward against the weight of his backpack. Rio always goes still like that when he's thinking hard, concentrating on something, trying to make a decision. I wish I knew what was going through his head right now.

When the bus turns a corner, two blocks away, I get a last glimpse of Rio, and he still hasn't moved.

# Fifteen

# MADDIE

Nighttime, again. Nights are better. No Laurel, no Emerson, no bus, no school. It's just Maddie and Bella.

And the moon. Outside Maddie's window, the moon looks like a white construction-paper smile pasted onto a black poster sky. Nighttime clouds drift across it, long and grey and silent as cats.

In the moonlight everything in Maddie's room looks soft.

The lines of her desk and chair and bookcase have all disappeared, with one shape melting into the next. Even her books have joined shoulder to shoulder, the light too dim to give any of them a name.

"What do you want to learn next, Bella?" asks Maddie.

At the sound of Maddie's voice, like always, Bella meows. Maddie doesn't want to laugh at Bella—she knows what it feels like to be laughed at—but it's just too funny to watch her meow. Bella's jaws open so wide that Maddie can see her little pink plastic tongue. And the sound isn't really like a cat, more like a person trying to be a cat: MEE-OWW.

Maddie pats Bella's head. "Maybe you could learn to talk."

Maddie knows that can't happen. Even if Bella wanted to talk she couldn't. Her mouth doesn't have the right shape to make all the sounds people do. But that's okay. Bella understands her, and she understands Bella.

Maybe Bella could learn to read the words in a book. Maddie could teach her that. The idea makes Maddie slide off the bed in a hurry, heading for the box in the closet where she keeps her old books, the baby ones with the fat cardboard pages and big letters and bright color pictures.

That's when Maddie hears the noise.

It's not a noise that makes sense, like the clear slam of a door. But Maddie thinks suddenly that this is not the first time she's heard it. Over the past few minutes—maybe longer—the noise has come two times or three times or more, and it's only now that she's paying attention. There is a faint odd tickling at the back of her neck, as if she has seen a shadow in a place it doesn't belong. Right away Maddie knows it. There is someone downstairs. There is someone in the house who doesn't belong. She's sure of it.

Maddie reaches out to take Bella into her arms. At the touch Bella is programmed to move her legs or swish her tail. Yet Bella stays quiet, stays still. So she knows it too. There's something wrong.

Again, the noise. There's no reason for a noise to come from downstairs—everyone else went to bed hours ago. What is it? Not quite a whisper. Not quite a footstep. Not a candy-wrapper crackle or refrigerator-door thump like when Dad makes a late-night snack. More like a breeze. Like the sleeve of a jacket brushing a wall. Like something felt more than heard.

Maddie's body freezes, like it has a million times before. But this is not like the first day of school, or a teacher asking her a question, or being left behind in a store at the mall. This is different, bigger. Maddie's face tightens. She presses Bella to her chest. What Maddie wants right now is to sink back onto her bed and make herself small, to hide under her blanket so she won't hear the noise again. What she wants more than that is to yell as loud as she can for Mom and Dad and Sadina. But Maddie knows what will happen if she opens her mouth: nothing. No sound will come out.

Maddie stands in the center of her room and doesn't move at all. She stares at a slice of white moonlight on the floor just in front of her feet. She starts to count, up to sixty and then over again and again, one number for each breath she takes. How many minutes have gone by? Three. Now five.

*Don't move, Bella. We can make it to ten.*

And all the time she listens.

No noise. No noise for ten minutes, at least, if her counting is right. It feels funny, this quiet. Not empty enough. Like it's holding its breath. But Maddie shakes off the feeling, because no noise should be good. It should mean that whoever was in the house is gone.

Maddie's body is telling her it doesn't have the power to move. Like when she was four and took a long walk with Sadina, then came back so tired she sank right down on the kitchen floor, stretching flat out, and Sadina said, "What's the matter, Maddie? Batteries low?" That has always made Maddie laugh. She is very far away from laughter right now. But the memory is like a hand stretching out to hold onto her. Maddie

lets it pull her all the way to the door and slowly, carefully, into the hall.

Sadina's bedroom is five steps down the hall to the right. Mom's and Dad's bedroom is just beyond Sadina's. To Maddie's left is the staircase. She doesn't mean to go that way. She doesn't even mean to look that way. But from the corner of her eye she sees him.

A shape, hunched over like he's carrying a secret. He crosses the hall at the foot of the stairs. He moves so quickly and so quietly, like the dark isn't even in his way.

What's he doing in this house at night? He shouldn't be here. He doesn't belong here now.

*Don't look up, please please don't look up.* She sees him for a few seconds, that's all, but time slows and unwinds and it might be hours that she's been pinned to the wooden floor here at the top of the stairs, in plain sight if he just happens to turn his head.

And then he does. He turns his head—and looks straight up at Maddie.

When he sees her, he freezes and stares. Maddie stares back. She can't look away from his face. His eyes are so wide and surprised. His mouth opens, but it seems like he can't push a single word out. Is he scared too? But that doesn't make Maddie feel better. It makes her feel worse.

He stretches his lips into a smile that doesn't look happy at all. Then he reaches one hand out to her, showing her what he's holding.

"I had to get this," he says finally, in a voice so low she can barely hear him. "But I didn't want to wake anyone up."

He waits.

But he must know she can't answer.

The silence drips into the space between them.

He puts a finger to his lips and whispers. "Don't tell anyone I was here. Okay?" She stares. He waits.

"Promise me. I need you to promise. Don't tell anyone I was here." The fake smile is gone now, and his voice is telling, not asking.

He puts one foot on the bottom stair, and Maddie feels her stomach rise right up into her throat. "If nobody knows, nobody gets in trouble. Promise me."

She can't speak or nod or even blink.

He keeps his eyes locked with hers. The foot comes back off the stair. Then he's gone, around the corner and out of sight.

There is one more noise, soft and this time perfectly clear. It's the click of a latch as the front door closes.

Maddie is not sure how this happens, but with her next breath she is back in her room, curled in her bed, the covers all the way up to her eyes. She has never left this place. She was never in the hall. She never heard a noise.

She tucks Bella under her chin. Through her window the moon keeps smiling from the black poster sky.

# Sixteen

# SADINA

There's a routine to breakfasts in my house. Mondays are bagels and muffins that Mom picks up at the bakery over the weekend. On Tuesdays, Dad makes pancakes and bacon. Wednesdays: Mom's waffles. Thursdays we're back to Dad for eggs and toast. By Friday, they're both worn out so it's usually cereal, but there's still a pitcher of fresh-squeezed orange juice to go with it.

Hearing all that, you might think my parents are passionate about cooking. You'd be thinking wrong. The truth is, dinners in this family, the kind where we all gather around the table over a home-cooked meal and "connect" with each other, don't happen very often. Between Mom and Dad working, getting Maddie to her sessions with the speech therapist, and bringing me to my basketball practices or music lessons or whatever, we're old friends with the pizza delivery guy. So I think they have this guilt thing about not feeding their kids properly. That's why they go all out with the breakfasts. Which is good. Not making my own breakfast means I can sleep in a few more minutes.

On Tuesday morning, routine jumps out the window.

It starts when I wake up. The scent receptors in my nose are all standing ready for the smell of bacon and warmed-up maple syrup. I'm up and dressed and out in the hall—my eyes only halfway open—before I realize: nothing. No stack-of-pancakes aroma floating up the stairs. That's weird thing number one.

Before I reach the stairs I pass by Maddie's room. As always, the door is wide open. Maddie's in bed with her eyes scrunched shut, almost like she's pretending to be asleep. Sort of cute, but Maddie's not just a night owl—she's also an early bird. She's always the first one up. So that counts as weird thing number two.

I don't find Mom or Dad in the kitchen. I track them down to Mom's office, where they're both standing in front of her desk and staring at it. The top drawer hangs open and tilted, like it's off its track on one side.

That, definitely, is weird thing number three.

"What's going on?" I ask quietly. This time, nobody jumps at the sound of my voice.

Dad takes a deep breath. "Sadina, honey, did you hear anything last night?"

"No. I just woke up."

"Nothing at all?" he repeats. He looks at me so hopefully that I'm starting to wish I had something to say, but I have to shake my head. I have no idea what he's talking about.

"We need to tell her," Mom says to Dad.

Now they both look at me, a long careful look like they're measuring my readiness for what's coming. My stomach takes a little dive. Dad's favorite expression goes through my head: Be careful what you wish for; it might just come true. I've been wishing I could find out what's going on with Maddie. Now that it's about to happen, there's a part of me that would like to be five years old and plug my ears.

"We don't need to panic about this, but it looks like someone might have broken into the house last night," Dad says, his voice deliberately slow and calm.

Okay, I did *not* see that coming. There's no mirror in this room but I can imagine the expression on my face right now. Probably just like when I'm a step behind the game and get faked out on the basketball court.

"Wait," I say. "Broken into?" It doesn't add up to me. Maybe it comes from too many bad TV dramas, but I'm thinking that if our house has been broken into, shouldn't I see a smashed window or two? All our stuff upended on the floor? Mom's computer isn't even missing.

"I checked all the doors and windows," Mom says, following my gaze around the room. "Nothing's broken, but the front door is unlocked. And I found my desk like this." She points to the dangling drawer.

"So someone breaks into the house just to go through your desk?" I'm following Dad's lead, acting calm and rational, but the truth is, this is very creepy. The idea that someone was in the house sneaking around, while all of us were sleeping, makes me feel shaky and vulnerable. "What exactly did you have in there?"

"It was pretty important," Mom says, casting a quick look at Dad. "And it's gone. Whoever was in here knew exactly what he was looking for."

That's when it hits me. I don't know why it took so long. In my mind I hear Rio and me talking on the bus yesterday on the way to school.

Me: *Mom had something in her hand. She stuck it in a drawer.*
Rio: *You've got to find out what it is.*
Me: *She probably locked the drawer.*

Rio: *That doesn't have to stop you…Midnight…Meet where we always do.*

Oh no. Rio. Oh no. You didn't.

"Mom, what was it?" My voice sounds strange and sharp, but Mom and Dad don't seem to notice. "What was in the drawer? Something about Maddie?"

Dad gives a quick, impatient sigh. "Sadina, I already told you. This has nothing to do with Maddie."

It's hard for me to let that go. "It really doesn't? You're not sending her away or anything like that?"

"Is that really what you thought?" Mom asks. She runs her fingers lightly down my cheek, but I can see she's too distracted to pursue my worries right now. "Honey, it was Flynn's phone."

"Flynn's *phone*? Why did you lock it in the drawer? I thought Flynn was supposed to pick it up today."

Mom just nods. It's like she doesn't want to get started, like telling this story is going to hurt.

"Mom. *Please.*"

Mom leans back against her desk, letting it support her, and finally she talks. "Last night, after you went up to bed, I found Maddie in the kitchen with Flynn's phone. She was just having fun, pushing buttons, and the phone started playing back some of his voicemail. I took it from her and turned it back off, but…I heard something."

"What?"

"It was from Kyle. Flynn's brother. Flynn mentions him sometimes. I guess Kyle is having a hard time. He got sick, got laid off from his job, can't pay his bills—so Flynn helps him out. Anyway, I just heard Kyle say a few words, but it sounded strange and it made me wonder what was going on." Mom shrugs. "I shouldn't have done it, but I played the whole message."

Wow. That's not like Mom. Whatever she heard must have sounded worse than strange.

"What was odd was that Kyle was practically begging Flynn to stop sending him money. He kept saying it was too risky. He said he would never forgive himself if Flynn got caught and lost his job and went to jail."

Mom is twisting her ring around and around on her finger. She's done talking, but I don't see what this all adds up to.

Dad catches my questioning look. "It sounded like Flynn is stealing money from the company and giving it to Kyle. It's called embezzling. And if that's true, Flynn's digging himself into some deep trouble."

Again, wow. This is crazy. I can't make this desperate, criminal Flynn I'm hearing about match up in my head with the funny, friendly Flynn I know, the one who rocks out on table tops and plays name games with Maddie and me.

"There's another thing," Mom says softly. "Flynn and I work together. There's a chance people will think I'm involved in this too."

"But doesn't the message on the phone prove it was just Flynn…?" My voice trails off. The phone is gone—and I'm back to Rio. I never thought it was possible to have this many thoughts in my head all at once, but in the passing of about two seconds I'm thinking *Rio, you idiot. Now I have to tell Mom and Dad you were the one who broke in here and took the phone. Now you're going to get in even more trouble. There's got to be a way around this. Rio, we've got to talk, now.*

I'm backing out of the office. I need to call Rio. Better yet, run over to his house to see him face to face. There's still time before school if I move.

"I can't believe Flynn would do this," Mom is saying. "We've put two years into this battery project. And now he's jeopardizing everything we've done." Her voice sounds so heavy, so disappointed. For the first time I see how hard this hits her.

"Sadina, if you could get Maddie her breakfast this morning, that would be a big help," says Dad. "We need to figure out what to do."

"You're not calling the police or anything?" I ask, my voice even edgier than before. Please, Mom, not yet. Five minutes to talk to Rio, that's all I need.

"It might come to that, honey. It's just, I've known Flynn for a while and it's hard to see what to do here." Mom looks at me carefully, searching my face for something. "I don't want to jump to any conclusions. I won't let him get away with anything illegal, but I need a little time to figure this out. Do you understand?"

Let's see. You have a good friend you've known for years and now you think he's done something wrong and you don't know what to do. Do I understand? Oh, Mom, you have no idea.

# Seventeen

# SADINA

Maddie is still in bed, but at least her eyes are open. I sit beside her, on the edge of the mattress, and brush her nose with one of her brown curls.

"You need to get up, princess," I say, trying to keep my voice calm. "Something happened last night and Mom and Dad have to deal with it. I don't have time to explain. I'll put some cereal out for you, okay? But I need to run over to Rio's for a minute. Tell Mom I'll be back in time for the bus."

Without a word Maddie pushes the covers back. That's all I need to see. In my own room I pull on my black jeans and the first sweater I touch in the closet—no time for fashion decisions now. As for my hair, it's clearly going to be a ponytail kind of day.

I check Maddie's room on the way downstairs. She's standing at the window, her back to me, looking out at a morning that's a gray wet streak.

"It's raining cats and dogs," I say lightly. Still no answer. I don't know what's up with her, but I can't stop to find out. In the kitchen I pull everything out at top speed: bowl, spoon, cup, cereal, milk, OJ. Then I grab an umbrella and I'm out the door.

I might as well not have bothered with the umbrella. Right away the wind wraps me in a rough hug and doesn't let go.

I fight it for three blocks, then turn the corner at Rio's street. No relief: somehow the wind shifts and keeps blowing the rain straight into my face. When I reach Rio's house—a plain two-story place with a brick front, pretty much a clone of every house on the street—I take the three steps up to Rio's front porch in one leap.

I feel like a fish pulled out of a pond, dripping and thrashing around as I try to get my umbrella turned right side out again. I lean on the doorbell, hard. There's a familiar scratching sound from the other side, and when the door opens the first face I see has a pair of gorgeous pale blue eyes surrounded by thick grey fur. It's Juneau, Rio's Siberian husky dog. He doesn't bark but he doesn't need to. He looks so much like a wolf that if you didn't know him, you'd probably cross the street so you wouldn't have to pass too close. But Juneau and I are old friends, and right now he's licking the raindrops off my fingers.

Mrs. Walker smiles behind him, looking not at all surprised to see me there. "Sadina, sweetie, you're soaked. I'll grab you a towel."

"Thanks, Mrs. Walker. Where's Rio? I just need to talk to him for a second before the bus comes."

"At the computer, I think," Mrs. Walker calls from the closet. She comes out with a gigantic blue bath towel that looks a lot like the one they use to dry off Juneau after he goes out in the rain. But it also looks and smells clean and anyway, with a lake forming around my feet, I'm not in a position to be choosy.

The Walkers have one computer—Rio's, really, because he's the only one who uses it—in the family room. Sure enough, that's where I find Rio. He's typing with one hand and holding a piece of toast with the other.

Rio looks up and raises his eyebrows at the sight of me, soaking and breathless with Juneau at my heels. He's so calm. After the morning I've had, that sends a spike of frustration straight through me.

"Rio, where's the phone?" I keep my voice low, because I don't know where Mrs. Walker is.

"What phone?" Rio hits a key and swings around to face me.

"The phone from my mom's desk. The one you said you could break in and get, remember?"

Rio stares at me like my words are being scrambled. I see absolutely no sign on his face that he has any idea what I'm talking about.

He shrugs. "How should I know?" There's enough coldness in his voice to remind me we didn't exactly part as best friends on the bus yesterday.

Okay, this is how it is. If there's one thing I know for sure after watching Rio battle his way from age four to fourteen, it's that he's not a great liar. And the look on his face right now says he's telling the truth: he really *doesn't* know what I'm talking about. I, meanwhile, am tired and mixed up and wet and cold, and I need a friend. The only thing I can think of to do is to tell Rio everything.

"I found out what Mom had in the drawer. It was a phone," I start. "And it's missing."

I want to keep the story in order and cover every detail, but in the end it just shoots out piece-by-piece, hard bits of fact mixed with soft bits of impression. There's the image of the desk drawer, hanging on one hinge. The relief of knowing all this had nothing to do with sending Maddie away. Then the weirdness of Flynn stealing money and sending it to his brother. And, through all of it, the sadness in Mom's voice.

Rio is quiet when I finish. He reaches down to Juneau, who's lying by his feet now, and scratches the dog's broad gray head. For a minute I'm scared. Maybe he's still mad at me. I doubted him yesterday. And I assumed the worst again today, storming in here and accusing him of sneaking into my house and stealing the phone. Why should he be there for me?

But when Rio finally looks up, swinging his hair out of his face, there's no anger or attitude there.

"Well, I wasn't the one who broke in and took the phone. So what really happened? This guy Flynn broke into your house and took it back?" he asks.

"That's what it looks like, I guess." And, I realize now, Mom and Dad probably figured that from the start.

"Without it, your mother's got nothing on him," Rio says.

I want to talk this out some more, but time's up. I can hear Mrs. Walker calling from the kitchen for Rio to finish up with his breakfast. And I've got to get back home so Maddie and I can make it to the bus stop.

Rio is already out of his chair and heading toward the kitchen. At the doorway he turns back. "Catch it, Juneau," he calls, and lobs the last of his toast across the room. Juneau's blunt jaws snap shut on the crust before it hits the floor. Juneau's excited now. He scrambles up, bumps his head hard on the desk, shakes it off and follows Rio to the kitchen. I almost smile as I trail after them—and it feels good to find something even remotely funny right now.

Two steps later I stop short. What did I just see? When Juneau gave the desk a bump, the motion must have shaken Rio's computer out of sleep mode. The screen is bright again, filled with the logo of a bright orange tiger holding a computer mouse in its mouth. I know that logo, and there's only one place it could come from: the software that Rio was looking at when we were at the mall.

The same software that Rio was accused of stealing from school.

A familiar refrain runs through my head: Oh no, Rio. Oh no. Tell me you didn't do this.

I've doubted him twice now. I can't do it again.

# Eighteen

## SADINA

The wind is at my back when I leave Rio. It takes me all the way home, cloaked in a stiff sheet of rain and cold and wayward leaves. Right now I would have preferred a fight, a chance to face the storm and punch my way through each gust.

Inside my front door I peel off my raincoat, shoes and socks. They're too wet and drippy to carry through the house, so I leave them, guiltlessly, in a heap under the coat rack.

I've got about five minutes before the bus shows up. Enough time to change into dry clothes, at least. This seems strange, worrying about catching the bus when my whole world is slanting sideways and trying to tip me off. The details of living life just make me keep moving, I guess. Even with all that's happening I still have to find something new to wear, towel-dry my straggling hair, squeeze three textbooks into my backpack, and round up Maddie.

Oh, yeah. Maddie. Where is she? I check the kitchen and that's when I notice that everything on the table is just the way I left it. Cup, bowl, spoon, cereal, they're all neatly arranged on the table. So she never made it down to breakfast.

"Maddie, where are you?"

My voice is louder than I meant it to be. I'm not really mad—with Maddie, that's not the way to get what you want—just tired of being on the edge. I take the stairs two at a time. Maddie's door is open and she's back in bed with the covers up to her nose. Her eyes are open but she's staring straight ahead, at something she obviously doesn't even see.

"Madeline Rose, what's the deal? You're making me late." I'm careful to keep my voice light.

She doesn't answer or glance my way. I touch the back of my hand to her forehead, like I've seen Mom do. She feels warm, but maybe that's just because my hand is still icy and damp from being outside. She could be sick. But the way she's acting makes me think of something else. Maddie gets like this—blank, withdrawn—when she's too stressed out. And what stressed her out? Me, of course.

I take the blame for that right away, like a quick kick in the stomach. I shouldn't have rushed off and left her here. What did I tell her before I left? "Something happened last night…" That was just dumb. Maddie can take a statement like that and blow it up like a balloon. Who knows what she's imagining.

"It's okay, Maddie," I say firmly. "Everything's fine." While it's easy to wind Maddie up, I don't really have any idea what to do to bring her back down. I try taking her little robot cat from the nightstand and putting it on her pillow. Maddie doesn't react, but it makes me feel better. "Don't worry, you don't have to say anything. I'll ask Mom if you can stay home today."

Mom and Dad are in the kitchen when I go back downstairs. When Dad sees me, he points to the empty cereal bowl and raises his eyebrows.

"I know, I know. She never ate breakfast," I tell him. "Maddie's sick, or something. She's doesn't want to go to school."

I'm not sure why I fall back on calling her sick, because I don't really think that's it. But one thing I do know is that Mom and Dad worry enough about Maddie. And somehow "sick" is better than "stressed out and not talking and one more reminder that Maddie has a problem you haven't solved."

Mom is already out of the kitchen and heading up the stairs. I trail behind her, trying to catch the disjointed words and directions she's tossing back over her shoulder.

"I'm staying home today anyway…so is your dad…have a lot to talk about…are those your wet shoes?…put them out on the porch before you go…do you have lunch money?"

The answers are "yes" and "yes" but Mom doesn't hear me. She disappears into Maddie's room and her voice goes soft and gentle.

I shrug and turn around—and then two things happen at once. Through the front window I catch sight of a traveling rectangle of yellow that can only be the bus. It's sending me a message I can't miss: the day is moving on, with or without me. At the same time, from about two feet away from me, the cordless phone lets out a ring as shrill and nasty as a smoke alarm.

I grab it and hit Talk, letting out a breathless hello.

Someone at the other end starts talking. I'm not sure who it is—his voice is breathless too, and quiet.

"I figured you wouldn't be going anywhere today, Elizabeth," he says.

Mom and I sound the same on the phone. Whoever this is, he's mistaken me for her.

"I'm not—"

He cuts me off. "If you're trying to decide what to do, just hear me out first."

There's no mistaking him now: it's Flynn. And whatever he's about to say, I'm absolutely sure I don't want to hear it.

"It's Sa—" I start again.

"Just *listen*." There's an edge to his voice, sharp and desperate. He barrels on. "I'm calling to say I'm getting out of here. Leaving town, and you won't be able to reach me. I'm sorry if all this falls on you. There's nothing I can do about that right now."

He pauses, but this time I say nothing.

"I'm just asking one thing. Don't tell anyone what I did."

Another pause, and again I stay quiet.

"Elizabeth?" His voice has gone deeper, darker. "That's all. Just don't tell."

He hangs up on me.

I look down at my hands. In a distant sort of way I notice that my fingers are trembling. I drop the phone. I can't let go of it fast enough.

It's the oddest thing. A little ripple is building in my stomach and making its way up through my chest, and all I want to do is get as far away from that voice as fast as I can. I've never felt this way before. It doesn't matter. I know exactly what it means.

The ripple—that's my instinct, tapping into the instinct of every animal on earth who knows this basic truth about survival: when you face something that's too big to handle, there's only one thing to do. You run.

# Nineteen

## SADINA

I don't have to run too far.

Dad is still in the kitchen, and I go straight into his arms and lean against him in a way I haven't done since I was ten. He hugs me tight for about two minutes, then takes me gently by the shoulders, settles me onto a chair at the kitchen table, and calls for Mom.

I spill out everything I can remember about the call.

Something changes in Mom while I talk. When she told me about the message on Flynn's phone earlier this morning, she looked blindsided. Flynn stealing all that money: She never saw it coming. She seemed hurt, too, that he would risk their work and their friendship. But all that is being replaced by something else. Her soft brown eyes turn hard and glinting, making me think of polished wood.

"So you're sure it was Flynn?" she asks. I can tell she's making an effort to take this one step at a time.

"I'm sure." I don't want any of this to be true. I've seen Flynn with Maddie, including her in a story and smiling her way, even when she never gave him one word back.

"It sounds like he's planning to get as far away from here as he can," Dad says to Mom. "And leaving you to cover for him. He must *really* be desperate."

Mom shakes her head. "I helped him get hired. I helped him find an apartment when he moved out here. And all this time he's been stealing research money right under my nose? I can't believe he had the nerve to sit at our table and eat *Thanksgiving dinner* with us," she says, tight-lipped, like that's the worst thing he's done so far.

There are a million things I want to ask right now, but I settle for the one that seems most obvious. "What are you going to do now?"

"Sadina, I don't know…" Mom starts, but her voice trails off. Her eyes lock with mine. She must see it in my face, how disoriented I am, because she reaches out to lay a hand against my cheek. Her touch is strong and steady. From her wrist I catch a faint pulse of rose, her favorite perfume. I've read that our sense of smell has the strongest power to bring back memories—more than sight or hearing—and right now that feels true. The scent of roses, together with Mom's touch, suddenly rocks me back five years.

I close my eyes and I'm nine again. That summer we went on a family vacation to Vermont. Mom and Dad didn't like driving on the highway, so we took an exit and headed west on Route 4. Dad always says the back roads are better, with more opportunity for something interesting to happen. He was right. We went only a few miles before the earth dropped out from under us. The road was passing over Quechee Gorge, a deep narrow notch in the planet's crust carved out by the river far below. Mom parked the car by a gift shop and we walked back to the middle of the bridge.

That was when a boy ran by, racing his sister to the other end of the bridge. He bumped me and I fell, my stomach pitching and my mouth opening to scream, I was so sure I would fly headlong over the rail and down into the gorge. There was no chance of it really, and Mom quickly caught my arm and pulled me back onto my feet. She laid her hand against my cheek and I breathed in that reassuring smell of rose. Then she walked me right up to the rail, holding my hand tight, and we looked over it together, down to where the rocks glared white in the sun and the river was a distant liquid mirror. I remember how the cliffs at either side seemed to shrink the world down to two dimensions. There was only one way for the river to go: straight ahead, flowing surely to its destination. The world down at the bottom of the gorge was far simpler than my own, which seemed filled with too many troubles and choices.

When I open my eyes, Mom is still watching me, and I swallow hard. How can I even ask Mom what she's going to do next? Right now, it looks like she has two choices.

Option #1, keep quiet and protect Flynn—which means he gets away with everything. Option #2, try calling the police, and see what happens. But we have no proof. Flynn's phone—with the incriminating message from Kyle—is gone. Either way, Mom could end up being the one blamed for the missing money.

It's like asking whether you'd rather be bitten by a lion or a tiger. Neither option sounds too good.

In the end, Mom decides there's one other thing she can do: She drives me to school.

She drops me off at the curb and squeezes my shoulder as I get out of the car. "I know it's hard, honey, but try not to worry. Dad and I will fix this."

I look back before I go inside and see that Mom is still parked at the curb, watching until the door swings shut behind me.

I've missed homeroom, of course. After signing in I head for English Lit, my first period class. I'm used to being in the halls when they're tangled with people, pulsing with shouts and the hollow clang of lockers. Now I can hear the shuffle and squeak of my own shoes. For the first time I'm moving slowly enough to notice that the metal locker doors are patterned with pits and dents. And Ms. Regen, the art teacher, must have created the room number signs for every classroom—Room 101, Room 102, all the way up the hall—because they all have the same gigantic loop in the R that she uses to sign her own name.

When I open the door to English Lit, Mrs. Weber glances my way and smiles. She gestures vaguely toward the class, motioning for me to sit down, never pausing in what sounds like a discussion of destiny.

Everyone is staring at me, wondering why I'm coming in late. I look around for an empty desk and chair. Mrs. Weber doesn't assign seats; she just encourages us to mix it up every day so we're always sitting with someone different. Paulie catches my eye and grins as he slides to one side of his chair, patting the other half. I ignore him and head toward the back of the room, where Monica is waving both hands to get my attention.

I slide into the seat next to her. "What are you doing back here?" I whisper. I've never seen her sit anywhere but in the very front row, close enough to see the board without her thick glasses.

Monica points dramatically at her eyes. "Contact lenses! Got them yesterday."

"Awesome," I tell her.

"So, now that we're all here," says Mrs. Weber pointedly, "let's get back to the forces of fate in Juliet's world." She's not very tolerant of talkers during class.

Monica shrugs and picks up a pencil. She writes a few words with her careful block print, every letter the exact same height. She rips the paper out of her notebook an inch at a time to keep the noise down and folds it neatly at the centerline. I'm just about ready to explode when she finally hands me the note and points at Rio.

Rio is sitting by the window, looking disgustingly cheerful. Apparently *he* caught the bus. "No worries in your world, Mr. Walker?" I mutter under my breath. I open Monica's note.

GOOD NEWS! RIO IS NOT GUILTY!!!

I look up at Monica. Her face is one big Julia-Roberts-size smile, showing as many teeth as she can. Rio's not guilty? I don't get it. I give her the classic eyebrows-raised palms-up gesture of confusion and mouth the word *"What?"*

Monica shakes her head impatiently and picks up the pencil again. Two solid minutes later, I get another note.

DUH! NOT GUILTY OF STEALING THE SOFTWARE!!!
HE PROVED IT!

I feel like an idiot but I do it again: *"What?"*

Now Monica looks like she wants to shake *me*. She bends over her notebook paper. While I'm waiting I try to tune back in to Mrs. Weber's discussion, just in case she calls on me, but

I can't seem to focus. Monica nudges me, handing me another creased note.

ACTUALLY CATALINA PROVED IT!!! SHE TOLD MRS. MERCER SHE WAS WITH RIO ON FRIDAY AND ALL HE DID WAS LOAD THE SOFTWARE, JUST LIKE HE SAID. SHE SWEARS HE DIDN'T TAKE IT OUT OF THE CLASSROOM. AND SHE SAYS SHE SAW A BUNCH OF SENIORS GO IN THERE LATER, SO MAYBE IT WAS ONE OF THEM WHO STOLE IT!!!

For the first time I notice that Catalina is sitting right in front of Rio. As I watch, she swivels sideways on her seat and rests an arm on Rio's desk, deliberately getting in the way of his note taking. If I was doing that to Rio—and I know this because I've done it—he would tease right back. Probably jab my hand with his pencil or just give my arm a shove. But all he does now is look at Catalina and smile.

Okay, something strange is going on here. I know I promised myself not to doubt Rio again, but still the fact is there, looming in my face: I saw that software on Rio's computer. And I just don't believe Catalina. If she was really with Rio after the computer-aided design class on Friday, Rio would have mentioned that right up front, when he was called to the principal's office. After all, if you're accused of a crime and you have an alibi, you'd say so, right?

"Why didn't he tell Mrs. Mercer that Catalina was there?" I hiss at Monica.

She starts to write again but I grab her elbow. "Just tell me!"

"Catalina says he was protecting her," Monica whispers with a happy little sigh. "He didn't want to get her involved."

Hmmm. Noble Rio. It's clear Monica thinks this is the most romantic thing ever. Maybe the principal—and everyone else—buys Catalina's story, but I don't. So here's what I want to know: Why is she lying for Rio? And why is he letting her do it?

The only person who can tell me that is Rio.

I desperately need to talk to him. To find out the truth about Catalina and to hash through this whole thing with Flynn's phone and the break-in. I'm used to bringing my troubles to Rio, and him bringing his own to me. Rio was the first person I turned to when Dad once talked about taking another job and moving the family to Michigan. And Rio and I spent every evening on the phone when his mother was in a car wreck and had to stay in the hospital for a month. We can talk for hours if we need to, until we pound the trouble from rock to dust.

The problem, now, is that I can't get Rio alone for a second. Between classes I trail him down the halls, but he's always ten steps ahead and in the middle of a pack of his friends.

And Catalina. She's always there too. At lunch I come up behind Rio to grab a place at the table before it fills up. Catalina is already at his side, their orange trays nudged against each other. Catalina has chosen the exact same thing for lunch as Rio, down to the little blue carton of whole milk and the chocolate-covered ice cream bar, when I know she only drinks skim milk and never eats ice cream. How cute, I think with a big eye-roll. That's when I notice they're holding hands under the table. At first I see it without making sense of it. Then finally it hits me that holding hands is something that boyfriends and girlfriends do.

Have you ever seen something or heard something that turns you completely numb? I remember Rio saw Juneau get hit by a car when he was still a puppy. Juneau flew about twenty feet through the air. Rio told me that somehow he couldn't move. People were running to Juneau's side but Rio said he felt paralyzed, like all his wiring just got disconnected.

Now I know exactly what he meant. I go through the rest of my classes on autopilot. I have never felt so completely alone.

# Twenty

# MADDIE

Maddie sits with her back against the wall, trying to tug the cuffs of her sweater over her clenched hands. It's cold up here. The cold is like a living thing, crowding her, and she shrinks herself as small as she can to avoid its touch.

At least it's not dark. Above Maddie's head there's a window. The light arches over her, cloudy with spots of dust that swim past her like fish. That's all she can do right now. Watch the specks of dust. And the dead mouse.

It's hard not to look at the mouse. The trap that caught it has flipped over so she can't see its head. Maddie is grateful for that. But there's still the soft white stretch of belly and a tiny whip of tail. On the other side of the mouse is a pile of camping gear. Maddie can see the dark blue plaid of a sleeping bag near the bottom. She wants the sleeping bag. She can imagine sliding it over her legs and sinking in up to her chin. But that means standing, unfolding herself to the cold, crossing the floor with telltale footsteps, and reaching right over the mouse to pull the sleeping bag out. Four things that Maddie cannot face. She's trapped just as much as the mouse.

She breathes on her hands, trying to warm them. Her fingers are cold and her nose is cold, and her legs are cramped from sitting still. Even her brain doesn't seem to be working. There's just too much to think about right now. It's easier not to think at all.

Maddie lets out a sigh. Bella is tucked against her sweater. When Maddie scratches behind her ears, Bella answers with a mechanical purr. Maddie shifts Bella onto her lap, setting the cat's four paws in motion. *Not yet*, thinks Maddie, running her hand down Bella's back until the cat lies still again. *We can't go anywhere yet.* Maddie needs more time. More time to decide if she can break a promise she never really made. More time before she's ready for the questions she can't answer, the words handed to her that she can't return.

Maddie lifts Bella up so that they're eye to eye.

*Talk to me, Bella,* Maddie whispers. *Talk to me, and we'll figure out what to do.*

# Twenty-One

## SADINA

When I was four years old, Mom says I had three favorite words: "I do it."

I wanted to tie my shoes and comb my own hair. I wanted to pour the milk into my cereal bowl and buckle myself into the car seat. Mom says it didn't stop there. When she was working at her computer, I would try to push her aside and take over the typing. When Dad was frying an egg, I'd grab for the spatula. They never say so, but it sounds like I must have been a total pain.

I remember it, sort of. I remember feeling like I had to try out everything and see if I could do it myself. Although my four-year-old brain didn't know how to put it into words, I think I just wanted to be ready—ready to fry my own egg and type my own emails in case some sort of disaster hit my world and left me all on my own.

As I get off the school bus, I'm thinking that all the skills I've learned since I was four years old should come in handy now, because my world is definitely collapsing and it feels like there's no one to deal with it but me.

I'm not sure what I expected to see when I got home. Cop cars parked in the driveway and detectives dusting the house for fingerprints, maybe. Instead I find Mom and Dad sitting at the kitchen table with coffee cups. The scene could be perfectly normal and every-day until I see their faces, which look like something out of a zombie movie.

I don't waste time on hellos. "What happened?"

"It's Flynn," Mom says simply.

"Flynn? You mean he confessed?" I feel a crazy impulse to laugh out of sheer relief, but Dad stomps that out with his next words.

"He didn't confess. In fact, he did the exact opposite." I've never seen Dad look so tired. It's like every word is an effort.

Mom squeezes his hand and then turns to me. "We sat here all morning talking about what to do. But there was never really any choice. I finally decided to call the lab director and tell him what happened. But Flynn beat me to it."

I have a bad feeling about where this is heading. I grab for the back of a chair to steady myself.

"I have to admit it, Flynn is smart," Mom says, but her voice is about as far from admiring as it can be. "According to the director, Flynn said I've been stealing money out of our research budget for years."

Smart is one way to put it. Evil genius is another. Flynn must have known that Mom would end up turning him in, however much she hated doing it. So he decided to strike first and get *her* in trouble. Everyone knows that old game. Paulie and Rick have been doing it to each other since they were old enough to talk.

"But it doesn't matter, right? I mean, there's no way they can believe him over you." I know I'm talking too fast but I can't stop. "Just tell them what really happened. Just tell the truth. Then this whole thing will be over."

"Honey, that's what I did," Mom says. "But…"

"But right now Flynn holds all the cards," Dad finishes for her.

Mom nods. "I'm sure he's covering his tracks. And what proof do I have? His phone is gone and all I can show them is a broken drawer on my desk."

"But what about the research money? Can't they trace it to Flynn, or his brother, or *something*?"

"Maybe. Or maybe Flynn played with the numbers to make it look bad for me. Either way, it looks like there's about a hundred thousand dollars that's not accounted for."

Whoa. This is getting completely crazy. This sounds like serious trouble for Mom.

"It's bad, Sadina," Dad echoes my thoughts. "The truth is, if the lab director believes Flynn and decides to prosecute…"

This time Mom finishes for him. "I could end up in jail."

Somehow I end up in my room. I'm not sure how I got here. I think I hugged Mom but I couldn't think of anything to say, and the next thing I knew I was sitting on my bed with my face in my hands.

Everything is moving so fast. Hard to believe what's happened since I woke up this morning: I found out someone broke into the house (creepy), I thought it was Rio (bad), I found out it wasn't Rio (good), I saw the stolen software on his computer (bad) but then Catalina told everyone he couldn't have stolen it (weird), I saw Rio holding hands with Catalina (bad and creepy and weird), and Flynn accused Mom of stealing a gigantic amount of money (super bad).

I reach for my pillow and hold it tight. I look all around my room, hoping for either distraction or inspiration, but there's no real chance of that in here. Kitten pictures on the walls.

Ruffles on the bedspread. A pile of *Magic Tree House* books under the bed. In other words, a million things that make this room look like it belongs to a little kid. None of this is me anymore.

In quieter times—like yesterday, maybe—I would go to my computer and design my dream room. The bed would be up against the wall or under the window. Either way, there'd be a fluffy rug at one side to greet my feet in the morning. I'd come up with the perfect color scheme, like sky blue for the ceiling and grass green for the floor. And I'd put Polite Convention posters all over the walls. There would be only one rule: absolutely no kittens. Those pictures would go to Maddie.

That's when I remember there's one person I left off my list of troubles. Maddie, who didn't go to school today.

I head to her room and stand at the doorway. Her blankets are bunched at the foot of the bed. There's a small stack of books on her nightstand—I can see from here they're all baby ones, like *Spot* and *Winnie the Pooh*—and on the floor a pile of t-shirts and skirts and leggings that didn't make it into her laundry bin. But no Maddie.

There's absolutely no good reason that my worry hormones should be firing up. Probably she felt better and just got tired of hanging out in her room. But anyway I move quickly, checking the rest of the upstairs. She's not in Mom and Dad's room, where she sometimes curls up on their bed. She's not in the bathroom. I even check the linen closet, though the bath towels and bed sheets are packed in so tight not even a mouse could fit in there.

Downstairs I bypass the kitchen without Mom and Dad noticing—it's easy, I'm way off their radar again—and search the living room and dining room and closets. No Maddie. It's a long shot, with the rain and the cold, but I look on the front porch too. Still no Maddie. We don't have a basement. We don't have a garage.

We do have an attic.

It's just not that easy to get to. I take the steps back upstairs two at a time and pull open the door to the linen closet. This time the wall of towels and sheets doesn't stop me. They're stacked on shelves that are hinged along one side, like a door, so all I have to do is swing the whole stack out of my way. At the back of the closet, a steep narrow staircase heads up into darkness.

When I get to the top I reach up, hands flat, and push open the trapdoor that leads into the attic.

# Twenty-Two

# SADINA

The first thing I see in the attic is a mouse.

When I push the trapdoor aside I'm blinded for a second, coming from dark into the dusty light. As soon as my eyes adjust, I find myself practically nose to nose with a tiny, pointed gray face. I'm not the kind of girl who shrieks at the sight of rodents or spiders, but it's so close I can't help it—I let loose a little yelp. The mouse starts, gives me a look that I swear is more annoyed than anything else, then turns its back on me and disappears behind a rusty brown file cabinet.

I step into the attic. Right away I'm glad I'm wearing a hoodie. It's cold, but I don't plan to be here for long. I rotate in place, scanning in each direction. The walls are lined with junk: a tangle of grey metal folding chairs, piles of old paperbacks warped into permanent comma-shapes, a cardboard box over-loaded with dishes and bowls and cups that don't match.

The one spot of pink is what leads me to her.

It's the tip of her sneaker, poking past the corner of a rickety chest of drawers—a loud advertisement that Maddie is here. I didn't realize I was holding my breath, but I let it out now in a long grateful sigh.

"Maddie?"

There's no answer, and the sneaker doesn't move.

"Maddie, I see you."

When she doesn't answer for a second time, I cover the space between us in three fast steps.

Maddie is wedged between the chest and the wall, with her knees drawn up and her hands in two small fists. No matter what I say she won't look me in the eye. I've seen her like this before—many times. But never with me.

I feel a hiccupy flicker of panic. For one brief second I have to close my eyes tight, squeezing back the tears that well up out of nowhere.

The tears aren't just for Maddie. They're for me too. The words sound awful and self-pitying, even just inside my head. Still, here it is: I'm tired of all this. I'm tired of Maddie's problems butting into my life. Why couldn't she have been by my side through this mess, instead of sitting, mute and miserable, in the attic? In my little fantasy world Maddie is twelve, not seven, and we sneak into each other's rooms late at night and talk about everything. We share our CDs and we borrow each other's shoes without asking. And we always cover each other's tracks.

In the cold reality of the attic, I let that fantasy freeze and shatter into a thousand pieces. It isn't going to happen. And standing here feeling empty and teary isn't helping either Maddie or me. I have to do something.

First, get Maddie out of here.

I was hoping all I would have to do is uncurl her fingers, take her by the hand, and lead her back down the staircase and into her room. In the end it isn't that simple. She won't get up, so I slide one arm around her shoulders and the other under her knees and manage to lift her. She's small for a seven-year-old, but she's giving me no help at all. I make it as far as the trap door, but there's no way I'll risk carrying her down those steep rickety stairs. I go down first. Then I talk her down slowly and gently behind me, one step at a time. It's like coaxing a cat down out of a tree: you can't lose your patience or your focus.

We make it to Maddie's room, and I sit down next to her on the bed. Whatever it was that led her up into the attic, it's clear she hasn't found any peace from it. She's still not talking. I want to put my arms around her but I don't—she wouldn't like it. Maddie's speech therapist says we're not supposed to push her to talk, so I can't ask her any questions. Her face is a smooth blank wall. No hidden messages there. So how am I supposed to figure out what's wrong?

One thing I know: I haven't heard Maddie's voice at all today. I remember talking to her a few times this morning before I went to school. Those conversations were pretty one-sided. All me and no Maddie. At first I thought I must have said something to upset her, blabbing something stupid in my rush to get to Rio's house. But what if it was something else? Now that I think about it, she was acting funny from the first moment I saw her, before I ever said a word. What could have stressed her out so badly that she would stay silent all day? Maybe something happened before I even got out of bed this morning. Maybe she woke up early—that's possible, she doesn't sleep much and she's usually awake at some crazy early hour anyway—and heard Mom and Dad talking about the break-in. That makes sense.

Of course, there's another possibility.

It hits me with a sharp little ding, like a game-show bell telling me I've got the right answer this time. It all comes together. Maddie, the night owl who wakes at the sound of a whisper. Maddie, who's tenser than I've ever seen her before. Maybe she heard something that happened much earlier—like during the night. Maybe Maddie heard Flynn breaking in.

I slide off the bed and swing around to face her.

"Listen to me!" I grab her shoulders. I actually have to hold myself back from shaking her, trying to jolt some response out of her little marble face.

"Did you see something last night? Is that it? Did you see Flynn?"

I'll never make it as a lawyer, I know—you're not supposed to put words in the mouth of the witness. But it doesn't really matter what I say. Her hands are curled back into fists and she is most definitely not answering.

The knowledge that this might have happened—that Maddie saw or heard Flynn in our house—is almost unbearable. I don't want to be the one to carry it. And so without thinking I decide to do the one thing I always do when my life goes crazy: tell Rio.

There are some problems with this. For starters, he's probably not feeling like we're best friends forever. After all, I've betrayed him twice: first, not standing up for him when the principal accused him of stealing the design software. And then I assumed right away that Rio was the one who broke in last night.

But maybe, just maybe, he owes me something too. There has to be a story behind the software going missing and Rio suddenly becoming this big Catalina fan. We've always shared everything, and now he's shutting me out.

"Maddie, can you wait here?" It sounds stupid, saying it—it's not like we're going to start having a conversation. But even when she's not talking, I know she's listening, and I don't want Maddie to think I'm walking out on her. "I'm just going to get my laptop. I'll be right back."

It takes less than a minute to grab my laptop from my room and get back beside Maddie. I take a breath, type in my IM to Rio, and hit Send.

**lady_sadie:**     rio, it's me

One Mississippi, two Mississippi, three Mississippi…I'm counting and I'm sweating…how long do I wait?

**lady_sadie:**     i need to talk to u
**lady_sadie:**     are u there?
**redriver494:**     *im here*

Okay, that's not quite as friendly as his usual breezy "what's up?" but it's an answer. That's all I need.

**lady_sadie:**     it's maddie again
**lady_sadie:**     she stayed home from school today
**lady_sadie:**     when i got home i found her hiding in the attic
**redriver494:**     *?*

That got his attention. I keep typing fast, desperate not to lose him.

**lady_sadie:**     she's not talking to me
**redriver494:**     *y not? whats she mad about?*
**lady_sadie:**     no, she's not mad at me, she just won't talk
**lady_sadie:**     i mean she CAN'T talk

I know Rio has a soft spot for Maddie, no matter how he feels about me right now. I'm counting on that.

| | |
|---|---|
| **lady_sadie:** | i really need ur help with this |
| **redriver494:** | *ok* |
| **redriver494:** | *want to come over?* |
| **lady_sadie:** | can u come here? |
| **redriver494:** | *no* |

No?

| | |
|---|---|
| **lady_sadie:** | why??? |

There's a ten-second pause. I can tell Rio's typing but not sending. Whatever his explanation is, it's taking too long.

| | |
|---|---|
| **lady_sadie:** | i don't want to leave maddie — it would be better if u could come here |
| **redriver494:** | *no, cant right now* |
| **lady_sadie:** | why??? |

I know I'm being rude and pushy but I don't care. This is more of Rio holding back from me and I won't let him keep doing that.

| | |
|---|---|
| **redriver494:** | *catalina is here* |

Okay, once again I am grateful for IM. All Rio gets of me are words on a screen. He can't see my face or hear my voice and that's a very good thing, because either one would give away the fact that Rio might as well have just pushed me off a cliff.

# Twenty-Three

# SADINA

When I see Catalina at Rio's house, the first thing I think of is a leech.

They're sitting side by side on the sofa, and Catalina is not letting any daylight get between them. She has one arm around Rio's shoulders, and it looks like you couldn't pull her loose without blood flowing.

Rio, I'm not so sure about. He's got his hands planted on his knees and his mouth is a thin straight line. He's not really the snuggly type. On the other hand, I don't think he's pulling away from her.

But it doesn't matter what I think or what I feel. What I have to accept is that Rio isn't just Rio anymore, he's one half of Rio-and-Catalina. Riolina.

"Hey, Reyes," says Catalina. "So your little sister is doing the silent thing again?"

How does she do that—in one sentence make me want to slap her? The silent thing. Right. Like it's Maddie's choice.

"It's really none of your business," I say. My voice is cold enough to frost the whole room. I don't want her to be part of this.

Something runs across Rio's face that I can't quite read. Whether it's impatience with me or with the whole situation,

I don't know. But this has to be awkward for him too. And I have to remember: I need his help.

I take my tone down a notch. "Rio, can we talk?"

Rio nods. "Look, I hope it's okay, I did something before you got here…"

Before he can finish, I hear a rattle and thump coming up behind me and the next second I'm bumped, hard, in the back.

"Juneau!" I turn around expecting to see the husky's blue eyes laughing up at me but it's not Juneau who's standing there. It's Paulie, his tall frame leaning lopsided in the doorway. "Oh, it's you," I say faintly.

"Lady Sadie, is that how you greet your knight in shining armor?" says Paulie. "Very classy."

"Knight in shining armor? What are you talking about?"

"Rio sent out the SOS and said you needed help. So here I am." Paulie bows low, twirling his arm in what he must think looks like a courtly flourish. "And look who I brought with me."

Paulie steps back from the doorway and pulls on someone's arm. I figure it's going to be his double, Rick, but I get surprised again: it's Monica. She flicks her fingers at me in an embarrassed wave.

I turn back to Rio, who's looking at me calmly with his eyebrows raised.

"You sounded freaked out," he says. "I thought we could use a little help."

And he was probably thinking it wouldn't hurt to have a few people in between Catalina and me. Well, maybe he's right, as much as I don't like the idea of spilling my troubles out in front of any more people.

For a minute no one moves; we're all just glancing sideways at each other as we try to decide what to do next. We must look like one of those frozen scenes in a natural history museum, the kind of exhibit where the stuffed zebra and the stuffed lion eye each other across the fake terrain, caught forever in the moment before chaos.

Of all people, it's Monica who kick-starts us back into motion. She brushes by Paulie, takes my hand, and sits me down across the coffee table from Rio and Catalina. Paulie trails behind her and folds himself onto the floor near her feet.

"So Maddie's not talking," Monica says. "Tell us what's going on."

I'm not used to Monica taking charge. The glasses with red-wire frames and tinted lenses that hide her eyes are gone, and the pale hair that she usually lets hang in her face is wrestled into a tight ponytail. Maybe this is the real Monica, and the one I see at school—the whisper-voice, block-print, stay-inside-the-lines Monica—is a secret identity she takes on to slide through her school days unnoticed.

I take a deep breath, not sure how much to say. This is my mother's story too, not just mine. But I have to make them understand why it's so important to get Maddie to talk, to tell what she's seen—and so I give them everything.

They let me go, all of them, from start to finish without interruptions—though Monica draws her breath in sharply when I reach the part about Flynn betraying my mom, and through the whole thing Rio's fingers drum out a rhythm on his knees, the way he always does when he's worried. Catalina keeps her eyes on Rio, like she doesn't want to give any sign that she's paying attention. While I'm talking,

Juneau clatters into the living room, takes just an instant to pick up on our mood, and then quietly plants himself at my side. I finish out my story with my hand deep in the fur at the back of his neck.

When I finally stop talking, Paulie can't resist an exaggerated look at his watch. "I guess we didn't get the condensed version, huh?" he teases, but at a glance from Monica he straightens up and gives my foot a sympathetic thump. "So what I'm hearing is this," he says. "If we can get Maddie to talk, she could tell the police she saw Flynn breaking in and it would prove your mom is innocent." That's pure Paulie, neatly pulling the most important point out of my tangled story and into the light.

"There's one thing here that doesn't make sense to me," says Catalina, who is still keeping up her leech impersonation. "I mean, I get that Maddie's too freaked out to talk to *you*"—she flicks a look at me, managing to imply that speaking to me would freak anybody out—"but why won't she talk to your mom or dad?"

Well, at least she deigned to join the conversation.

"Before I came over here," I say, carefully directing my answer to everyone but Catalina, "I told Mom and Dad about finding Maddie in the attic, and they both tried talking to her. That's what makes it so bad—she's just not talking to anyone, and that's never happened before."

Rio shifts under Catalina's arm. It seems to me—and okay, I know sometimes we see what we want to see, whether or not it's really there—that he nudges her aside just a bit, sending one elbow out to give himself some space. "You have to remember," he says, "she's scared. I mean, it's not like she's doing this on purpose. It seems weird to us but she really can't talk."

Inside my head I thank Rio for seeing it Maddie's way for a second. Even I forget, sometimes, how scary and frustrating this must be for her.

"The point is," Rio goes on, "she can't just turn it on or off because someone tells her to." Rio never looks Catalina's way as he says this but I get the sense, again, that there's some kind of undercurrent going on here—a message being sent that only she is supposed to hear.

Catalina lifts her arm off Rio's shoulder and deliberately gets busy brushing back her hair and rearranging herself on the sofa—a solid foot away from Rio's side. Well, *that* was real enough—not just my imagination. I don't know what's going on, but the charge between the two of them right now is definitely not a positive one.

"Well, if Maddie's not going to talk, then we're really just wasting our time, aren't we?" Catalina says.

Monica flashes her a "can't believe you said that" look, but Catalina shakes her head.

"No, listen. What I mean is, you're all looking at this the wrong way. What's the point of trying to get her to talk if you know it's not going to happen? Come on, it's obvious, right?" She looks around the room, challenging us, but no one gets where she's heading. "Okay, I'll spell it out for you. She doesn't have to talk. Just ask her what happened and tell her to write it down. Case closed."

Paulie sits up straight, giving me a grin. "Yeah, that's perfect. Right, Sadina? Maddie can write, can't she? Or type? Just let her answer that way."

I shake my head. "It's not that easy." I know what it sounds like: I'm shooting down the idea because it's Catalina's. But it's the truth. I pause, not really wanting to explain. Like

I said, I don't like telling people about Maddie's problems. But everyone's eyes are on me, waiting. I have to try.

"It's not just about talking." For some reason my voice comes out shaky. I take a breath and start again. "You should see Maddie in school. Her teacher knows she can't talk, so he'll ask her to point to the right answer, and she can't even do that." I drag out another memory, a bad one. "There was this time my uncle visited. We hardly ever see him, so Maddie didn't know him at all. He tried really hard with her, and he asked her about twenty times to wave goodbye when he left, but she couldn't do it. He didn't get it. I think it really bothered him."

"It was his own fault," Rio says. "You're not supposed to push her. It just makes it worse for her."

He's right. The more you try to get Maddie to talk, to smile, to nod—anything—the more she'll withdraw. Rio has been around her long enough to know that firsthand.

"That's okay," says Monica, with another quick look at me. "We won't do anything to make it worse. If we give her a little time, maybe…?"

"You don't have time," Catalina says flatly. "Not if you want to keep Sadina's mom out of jail."

"Harsh, Catalina. But true." Paulie nods his agreement. "But we don't have to be firing questions at Maddie. We can find another way."

"Of course we can," says Monica, a bit too cheerfully.

The silence that follows makes everyone shift and avoid each other's eyes. Then Paulie slowly raises his hand.

Monica shoves his shoulder. "Just say it, stupid. We're not in school."

Paulie shrugs. "I thought of something. I have this friend who used to stutter. He couldn't get half his words out. I swear it hurt just to listen to him." Paulie's voice is quiet, almost shy—a sharp U-turn from his usual over-loud delivery. "But when he sang…it was awesome. It was perfect."

Rio snorts like he can't help himself, and the rest of us have to laugh. "Paulie, come on, you really think Maddie's going to *sing?*"

Paulie shrugs again, like he doesn't care that we're laughing, but I see the hurt look that flits over his face. "You got something better?"

"I don't know. Plant a bug in her room in case she talks to herself?"

It's Paulie's turn to roll his eyes.

"Okay, enough!" Monica claps her hands, the sound as loud and sudden as a door slamming shut. It's such a not-like-Monica thing to do that everyone's attention snaps to her. She narrows her eyes at each of us. "New rule: no more busting each other's ideas. Everyone can say what they want and no one is allowed to make fun of it."

"Good call, Monica," says Catalina, and for a second I think she's being sarcastic, but she goes on: "That's the only way we're going to get anywhere. I for one don't want to be here all day, so let's not tear each other apart."

Rio turns to her with a nod and a smile, a real one.

I have to look away. I lean over the side of my chair to pat Juneau, who is now lying flat with his head on his paws. "What do you think, boy?" I say quietly, stroking his wide back. "You have any bright ideas for us?"

Juneau lifts his head and gives me a serious stare, like he's considering the question. Rio laughs—and I'm embarrassed by how glad I am to have his attention back on me.

"Hey, we could send Juneau in to talk to Maddie," Rio says, grinning. "I bet he could get something out of her."

Paulie, of course, runs with it. "You up for it, Juneau? Want to be a detective dog? An undercover canine? A mutt with a mission?"

"Um, you know what I said about not busting each other's ideas?" Monica says. "It's over. That was just dumb, and we need to get serious."

The stress must be getting to us: Paulie and Rio start laughing harder. In a way I don't want it to end—the sound is just what I need right now—but I shoot my hand out like a stop sign, asking for silence. "Maybe it's not so dumb," I say. "I mean, Maddie really does like Juneau, and she might talk to him. But I was thinking, what she likes more than anything is Bella."

"Who's Bella?" asks Catalina.

"It's her robotic cat," I tell her. "She talks to it all the time."

"She thinks it's real," Rio adds. I wait a beat—that's not the kind of ammunition I want to give Catalina—but all she does is raise her eyebrows.

"So can this cat record stuff?"

"It could," I say slowly. "But even so, we need a way for it to ask Maddie the right questions—about whether she saw Flynn."

*A way to ask Maddie the right questions.* To make this work, we would have to do more than record stuff. Bella would have to be able to talk to Maddie. Talk to her and ask her questions in a way that makes sense. In other words, talk to her *like a person would*.

Rio and I look at each other. All around me everything seems to slow and fade, and for a second all there is in the world is the two of us, looking into each other's eyes. I know we're remembering exactly the same thing.

Maddie *did* already say the cat could think.

# Twenty-Four

## SADINA

"**W**hoa," says Mr. Jaworski. "You want to do *what*?"

"Program this cat to talk like a human," repeats Rio, pushing Bella across the desk.

"And we're kind of in a hurry," adds Monica. "We need to get started, like, now."

It's Wednesday morning, ten minutes before school even starts, and we've pulled Mr. Jaworski out of the teachers' lounge and into the computer-aided design classroom. He tilts his chair back—way back—and balances both sneakered feet on the edge of his desk. He's smiling at us through his beard but not—I think—laughing at us.

"Whoa," says Mr. J. again. "Tall order."

I've made everyone promise not to spill out the details of what's going on. We've told him this is urgent but not exactly why. But it must be obvious, the tension we all feel. Monica's hair is still up in a ponytail that clearly has not experienced a comb in twelve hours. Paulie and Rio most definitely have not changed their clothes since our meeting ended yesterday. Catalina hasn't even mentioned that everyone else is a mess.

And me, well, my body may be here but my mind is not. I think of Maddie, in her bed, still not talking, not even to protest when I said I was borrowing Bella for the day. I think of

Mom, at home for the second day in a row. For Maddie's sake, of course, but also because she has nowhere else to go. She got a call from work—from the legal department—telling her not to come to the lab.

Though I haven't said a word yet, Mr. J. looks straight at me, like he senses I'm the one with something at stake here.

"I'm assuming you have some ideas about what's involved," he says.

Rio jabs me with a not-so-subtle elbow. We hear some variation of that line every day in Mr. J.'s class: "I'm assuming you have a reason to think this is possible," or "I'm assuming you did some research before you took that approach." Usually, it's no. But today, we're ready.

I slide my backpack off my shoulder and pull out a sheet of paper covered with Monica's neat print. Mr. J. takes it from me. I watch his eyes. He reads it over three times, his chin propped on one hand, running his thumb up and down the side of his beard.

*What We Need Bella To Do:*
1. Understand what Maddie is saying.
2. Talk to Maddie like a human would.
3. Record the conversation so we can hear it later.

I think it's a pretty good list. I lean against the desk, holding my breath, like I'm waiting for Mr. J. to say that my homework gets an A.

What I get is not quite what I hoped for.

"Not bad." He slides his feet off his desk, pulls his chair up close, and smoothes the paper flat in front of him. "So what does all this mean?"

Before any of us can answer, the bell rings for homeroom. Mr. J. gives us a look, eyebrows raised. Nobody moves. "Okay," he says. "Stick around for a few more minutes. I'll write you each a pass."

I'm not going to waste any time. "The third one, recording the conversation." I point to the list. "That's the easy one, I think. We're not too worried about that."

Mr. Jaworski nods. "Agreed."

"And the first one," I go on. "Programming Bella to understand what Maddie's saying—"

"That's called speech recognition," Rio breaks in. "I looked it up online. There's software out there that can do it. You just talk into a microphone, and it's pretty good at recognizing what you say. It's supposed to get better the more you use it."

"So that leaves number two on your list," says Mr. J. "Get a robot to talk like a human. No big deal, right?"

We all stare at Mr. J. until the corner of his mouth twitches.

"Bad time for jokes, Mr. J.," Catalina shoots back.

"Hey, laughter is our only really effective weapon," he answers mildly, then smiles as Catalina squints at him. "That's a quote. I don't know who said it first. But actually, having a conversation with a robot may be less of a big deal than you think. Any of you ever heard of something called AI?"

Paulie raises his hand, and in a replay of last night, Monica shoves his shoulder. "Just *say* it, Paulie!"

"Okay, so, Monica and I did a bunch of research on this last night, and AI kept coming up," Paulie says. "It's artificial intelligence."

"Which doesn't mean there are computers that can actually *think*," Monica explains, and I flash back to Maddie exploding into my room, telling me Bella is real and can think for herself.

"It just means you can program them so they talk to you, answer your questions, stuff like that."

"It's hard to do," Paulie adds. "I tried a couple of the programs online. Some of them give you really weird answers— they don't sound human at all."

"But it's *possible*," I say, a little too loudly because I want it to be true. "Right, Mr. J.?"

The classroom door opens behind us, making me jump. It's two guys who are in Mr. J.'s first-period class. Mr. J. points them back toward the door.

"Out," he says. That pulls a grin out of both of them. They do an about-face and glide out. "Not too far!" he yells after them. "Just wait in the hall. Class is starting late today."

Mr. J. props his feet back up on the desk, ignoring my question.

"Tell me this. When you design this robot, what's most important to you? What has to happen to make this work?"

"Meaning…what?" I ask.

"Meaning, for example, do you have all the time in the world to get it done?" Mr. J. raises a hand to keep us quiet. "I know, I know. This is urgent. So one thing about this design is that it has to happen fast." He points at Monica. "Make a list. What else?"

"Moolah," Paulie says right away. "Dough, bucks, greenbacks, dead presidents—"

"Okay, shut up, we get it," Rio says, punching Paulie's shoulder. "Money. We don't have a lot of it. So this has to be cheap."

"Good. Anything else?"

There is one other thing. The one thing that will matter most to Maddie. "It has to look like a cat," I say firmly. "No matter what we do, it still has to look like Bella."

I look over Monica's shoulder at the new list.

*What's the Best Design?*
1. Fast
2. Cheap
3. Still looks like Bella

Mr. J. reads it out loud. "Tall order," he says for the second time. "And while you're at it, could the robot maybe tell us the meaning of life? If you'll excuse the joke, Catalina."

"So you don't think we can do this?" Catalina's voice is sharp.

"I never said that. But it won't happen in a day." Mr. J. looks at us one by one. "I can stick around after school. How about you?"

# Twenty-Five

# SADINA

Every day for the rest of that week and into the next, I take the late bus home from school. And every day when I get off at my stop the first thing I notice is that my house looks different.

It's not something you can touch. I mean, it's not like somebody smashed a window or slashed the car tires or spray-painted something nasty on the front door. It's an inside thing. It's a feeling rising from the pit of my stomach that says nothing is safe anymore. I can go in the house and close the door behind me and shut out the world for a while. The trouble is, all the problems are inside with me.

At the heart of it all is Mom. When she first told me that Flynn had betrayed her and blamed her for all the missing research money, I worried that she'd be behind bars the next day. Instead, the hours and days have dragged with no word from the lab director or from the police. Mom says that doesn't mean they think she's innocent—more likely they're investigating the case and building up the evidence. In the meantime, she hasn't been allowed to go back to work, and I can tell it's making her crazy. The kitchen table has become her home base, where she sits with Dad and talks and talks and keeps making more coffee while their cups are still half-full.

The problem with Maddie follows me into every other corner of the house. There's no place I can go to hide from it. Maddie's been to the doctor's office and the therapist's office but nothing has changed. She's still not talking to us. When I go into her room it feels as stuffed and heavy as a suitcase, filled with all the words she can't say.

And then, of course, there's Rio. I haven't forgotten what I saw on his computer: the same design software that someone stole from school. I've put that problem on a shelf in the back of my mind because, the truth is, I don't know what to do with it right now. What makes it more complicated is how much everyone — not just me but also Paulie and Monica and Catalina — has started to depend on him while we work on turning Bella into a talking cat. Through every frantic meeting with Mr. Jaworski, through every circuit that shorts out and computer code that we don't know exactly how to write, it's Rio who shrugs it off first. He's the one who gets up again and prods the rest of us to look for another way. I know he loves Maddie and so maybe it's all for her and not for me, but one thing I'm sure of: every time he swings his bangs off his face and looks straight at me, my heart sends a message to my brain that I couldn't get through this without him.

So when I get off the bus on Thursday, after seeing my friends (plus Catalina) every day for a week, it feels strange to be alone. Stranger still that I'm the one who insisted on it being this way. In my backpack is the prototype — that's what Mr. Jaworski calls the redesigned, new and improved Bella — and today I'm going to give it back to Maddie and see what happens. And though everyone wanted to be with me, I can't risk her being silenced by a crowd of watchers. This is something that Maddie and I have to do on our own.

But I don't even make it to the front door before things start to go wrong.

The garage door opens like a stage curtain, revealing Scene One: Mom and Dad in our car, backing slowly down the driveway.

I wave at them to stop. Dad rolls down the window. "Sorry, honey, we're running late. We need to get going."

I don't move yet. "What's going on?"

"We've got an appointment with James," Mom says, leaning across Dad so she can see me. James is her lawyer. Mom has had meetings with him a bunch of times already, so I don't see why's there's a big hurry for another one.

"Where's Maddie?" I ask. All that matters to me right now is getting Maddie together with Bella.

"She's fine, she's in the house," Mom says quickly. "Waiting for you. You should head in."

"Do you have to go?"

Mom and Dad exchange a glance. I'm sure they're wishing I were five years old again and would just do what they say.

"We'll talk about it when we get back," Dad says, sliding the gearshift out of neutral.

I shake my head and put a hand on the car door to stop him. "Look, this thing with Bella we've been working on, it's done." I unzip my backpack and pull out Bella, who looks pretty much the same except for a box on her back that holds some extra electronics and a cable that can attach to a computer. "I have to try this out with Maddie now. You should be there."

I've told Mom and Dad my theory that Maddie might have seen Flynn break into the house, and that we might be able to use Bella to get Maddie to talk, but I don't think they have much faith in either idea. "Mom," I push on, "if this works, it'll *prove* Flynn is lying."

Another parent-to-parent look that makes me feel, again, like a stubborn little kid.

"Sadina, I have to get to this meeting," Mom says finally. "The company's attorneys are going to be there. We'll be finding out whether they're pressing charges against me, and whether…"

Mom trails off, but I know where that sentence is heading. They'll be finding out whether Mom is going to jail. Mom reaches out a hand to me, and I recognize right away that this is my big moment, my chance to let her know I'm okay with all this, that she doesn't have to worry about me too.

Which makes the next words out of my mouth sound like the most horrible thing I've ever said.

"Fine. Just go."

No goodbye, no good luck, no I love you. Just bare and plain and dry, like bones—but behind my words is a swirling twister of every bad emotion I can think of. Frustration that I can't make them understand how Bella might be the key to proving Mom's innocence. Fear that Mom is in trouble she can't get out of. And worst of all, shame that I can't give Mom the support she needs right now. I let go of the car door, but I don't touch her hand. I just step back, out of their way.

The car idles while Mom and Dad stare at me like I'm someone they don't know. Then Dad hits the gas pedal and they roll down the driveway and into the street, moving forward now like a fish caught in a current, around a bend and gone.

The garage door rumbles shut behind them. End of Scene One. And Scene Two, I know, opens with me in Maddie's room. I have no idea how that's going to play out.

# Twenty-Six

# MADDIE

**B**ella looks funny.

There's something on her back, something that doesn't belong. It's a box, and it's held in place by three stripes of black tape that circle over the box and under Bella's belly. Bella must hate that. Maddie wants to pull it right off.

But Sadina says don't.

Maddie is sitting on the floor with her back up against her bed. Bella is on her lap, and Sadina is kneeling beside the bed with one hand on Maddie's arm, as if she expects Maddie to run away.

"Don't take that box off," Sadina says. "It's something really special, Maddie." Her voice gets quiet and careful, like she's about to tell the most amazing secret in the world. "You know how Superman has those laser eyes? And Spiderman's got the web, right? Well, this box gives Bella her super power. It turns her into…" Sadina's voice drops all the way to a whisper. "… Chattercat."

Maddie takes a quick sharp breath. With every inch of her body she wants to ask Sadina what that means. But she doesn't need words. Sadina sees the question in her eyes.

"Chattercat can talk to you, Maddie."

Maddie's hands curl tight around Bella, and slowly she turns to meet Sadina's eyes.

Without looking away, Sadina drops one shoulder, letting her backpack slide to the floor. She shuffles her hand inside it and pulls out another small box. It has a screen on it, like a computer but small, and a cord hanging from it like a mouse tail. Sadina reaches out for Bella and she's moving slowly, so slowly, as if she thinks Maddie will be afraid. But Maddie feels a buzz beneath her skin that has nothing to do with fear. Because now it's real. Now, finally, Sadina believes that Bella can talk.

Maddie lets Sadina plug the cord into the box on Bella's back. Sadina points to a button and Maddie pushes it with a finger that she can't keep steady. The screen lights up, glowing as blue as Bella's eyes.

"Hi, Chattercat," says Sadina, loud and clear.

And as quick as a person could answer—quicker, maybe, Maddie thinks—Bella's answer shows up on the screen: "Hi right back at you."

Maddie closes her eyes. It's all she can do. From somewhere in the room, maybe still by the bed, maybe far off by the door, Sadina is saying something. "Not right away…you have to… gets better…" But to Maddie it's a stream of words without sense. All her head has room for is the fact that Bella has really and truly found a way to talk to her at last.

Long after the room is quiet again, Maddie opens her eyes. Sadina is gone. Maddie scratches Bella gently behind the ears and, just like always, Bella purrs.

"Hi, pretty Bella," Maddie whispers.

She watches the screen.

"Bella, it's me, Maddie," she says. The sound of her voice is dry and dusty, like a book that's been left on the shelf too long.

No answer.

That's okay. It's her own fault, Maddie is sure of that. She hasn't talked to Bella for such a long time, and now Bella doesn't know what to say.

One more time. "Hi, Bella," she says as softly as she can. "Talk to me."

Maddie stares and waits and stares and waits, but the screen shines on, blue and blank and empty.

# Twenty-Seven

# SADINA

"All of you," says Monica, "are making me crazy."

All of us—the Chattercat team—are in my kitchen, and everyone's talking at once.

An hour ago, when I let Rio know that the Chattercat had failed, he rounded up everyone else—Monica, Paulie, and Catalina—and somehow got them here to my house. Now we're jammed in the kitchen: Rio sitting on the floor near the drawer where Mom hides the snacks, Catalina leaning against the counter with her apple-red nails carefully splayed out in front of her, and Monica and Paulie and me at the table where the Chattercat lies in pieces. If Maddie came through the door right now, she wouldn't recognize her Bella.

We've got to get the cat working. We're pretty much agreed on what went wrong: Maddie's voice was too quiet for the cat's microphone to pick up. So that has to be fixed. We just all have a different idea how it's going to happen. If Paulie is right and we need to redesign it completely, it's going to be a long night.

I catch Monica's eye. "I'm going to order some pizza," I tell her. No one else hears me or notices me as I get out of my chair and slide out of the kitchen. I head for Mom's office, but it's not really the phone I'm after, it's just the quiet.

I need to think. And it's not about the Chattercat.

Here it is, straight and simple: I can't stand wondering anymore if Rio stole the design software from school. Worrying about it is jumbling up my mind. I can't stop thinking about it when I look at him. I can't stop thinking about it when I *don't* look at him. There's a part of me—the honest part—that says I should just go to the principal's office tomorrow and tell him what I think is true. In my head I have the bad ending to that all worked out. I tell the principal that Rio has the software on his home computer—but no one believes me and I lose Rio forever. After all, that's just what happened to Mom. She told the truth about Flynn, no one at work believed her, and now she and Flynn will never be friends again. And she might end up in jail.

Then there's the other part of me—the friend part—that says I owe it to Rio to talk to him first and give him a chance to confess it on his own. I can think of a bad ending for that one too. He denies it, he hates me, and I lose him forever. And *he* ends up in jail.

This is hard. It's impossible. I want to be angry at Rio for making me so confused. But he's the same guy who stayed by my side through all this mess with Mom and Maddie. Even when it seemed he would rather be glued to Catalina. I can't walk away from that.

I head out of the office. And slam into Rio on his way in.

"What's taking you so long?" he says, rubbing his chin where I bumped it. "Can't decide if you want anchovies? Catalina hates them, if that helps."

"Thanks for the tip," I say, but my heart's not in it. I'm not in the mood for jokes. I take Rio by the arm and guide him to Mom's chair. He stares at me as I perch on the desk in front of him.

"We need to talk," I say flatly.

I've read all the teen magazines that say if you want a relationship to work, you don't start a conversation that way. It sounds too much like there's trouble coming, and the person you're talking to will want to run in the opposite direction. Sure enough, Rio narrows his eyes at me and crosses his arms.

"I'm just going to say it." I feel like a balloon that someone stuck a needle in—everything on the inside is going to find its way out in a rush, and there's no stopping it. "I saw that design software on your computer. And I'm not saying you stole it—I mean maybe I'm wrong, maybe you didn't—but I saw it there, and I know you wanted it, and I know you can't buy it, so I couldn't figure out where else it could come from except from school." I keep my eyes down, looking at Rio's feet in his big Converse sneakers, because I can't stand to see whatever might be in his face. I finish in a voice that's not much more than a whisper. "I don't want to get you in trouble."

Not being able to look at Rio's face is a problem. I have no idea what he's thinking right now. All I can do is keep staring at his feet. I want to give myself a kick, make myself into a person brave enough to say something and then look at the consequences eye-to-eye. But I'm just too scared to find out what I might have lost.

When Rio finally speaks, he says the last word I expected to hear. "Catalina."

His voice is so quiet I'm not sure I heard him right. "What?"

"Catalina."

I spin around, expecting that she's done her sneak-up-as-quiet-as-a-snake routine and is listening to us from the doorway. But no one's there. So what's going on? What does Catalina have to do with this?

Now I have to see his face. But as soon as I look at him, Rio turns away and walks over to the window, looking out and giving me nothing but his back.

"Rio, what? What about Catalina?"

"I was hoping I was never going to have to explain this to you," Rio says. The fingers on his left hand tap a crazy fast rhythm against his leg. "You're going to think I'm a total loser."

I can't imagine a world where I would ever think that. I want to tell him so. But I can't find the right words fast enough, and Rio keeps talking.

"I didn't steal the software," he says. "I just want you to know that." I let out a breath that I didn't even know I was holding in. I didn't realize how terribly I wanted to hear him say those words. I believe him right away, absolutely and completely.

"Here's the weird part," Rio goes on. "Catalina stole it. She knew I'd get the blame because I was the last person to use it, and everyone knew I really wanted it. And that's what happened. Everyone thought it was me." Rio's voice sounds strangled, like it's hurting to come out of his throat.

"So this was the deal. If I told anyone that Catalina stole it, she said she'd just deny it. No one would have believed me anyway. But if I kept quiet, Catalina said she'd make up a story to keep me out of trouble. Which she did."

Slowly Rio turns away from the window. He looks right at me, which I think is maybe the bravest thing he's ever done. Much braver than I could be. His face looks so mixed up and sad, and it hits me that all this time I've thought I was the only one in the middle of trouble, while Rio has been just as messed up as I've been. *You could have told me*, I think, but of course that's not even true. Because I was one of the people who didn't believe him. "Rio, I'm sorry," I say, but he shakes his head.

"Let me finish. It gets weirder." Rio gives the smallest smile, really nothing more than a twitch of his lips. "You won't even believe this. Catalina said I owed her something for keeping the blame off me. Which sounds twisted now but, I don't know, for some reason it made sense when she said it. All she wanted me to do was go out with her a few times." He flicks me a quick look, and it's all I can do to keep my face blank. "It just seemed like the easiest thing to do. I really didn't want to get in trouble over this. And, Sadina, I know this makes me sound like the biggest jerk ever, but I really did want that software."

I should be raging mad at Catalina for all of this. I should be disappointed with Rio for going along with her lies. And I am, a bit. But that's not the loudest thing going through my head. This is it: Rio doesn't really like Catalina. Of course, not, how could he? How could I ever have thought that? There's a rising little bubble of happiness that threatens to burst right out of my mouth, but I stuff it back down. Now is not the time. I need to hand back to Rio some of the strength and support he's been giving me.

"We can fix this, Rio," I say. "We just need to tell someone the truth. I won't let her do this to you."

Rio stares at me like he can hardly believe I'm on his side. I wish he never had to doubt that. Without thinking, because it seems like the only right thing to do, I cover the space between us and put my arms around Rio. I feel him sigh, and I know exactly what's going through his head. Troubles are never so heavy when you've got someone else to help you take the weight.

"I know the first thing we need to do," I whisper. "We need to order that pizza."

Rio's shoulders give a little shake.

"Yeah," he whispers back. "And make it extra anchovies."

# Twenty-Eight

# SADINA

"**Y**ou are *so* not worth it, Rio Walker!"

The classroom door opens with a rush and a bang and out flies Catalina. She strides straight toward me and Paulie and Monica, and I take a quick step back, because honestly she looks a little scary and I'm not sure what she intends to do. But then she looks up and I realize she doesn't even know where she's going. She turns her head so we can't see her face and takes off down the hall in the opposite direction, her heels hitting the floor like two wild jackhammers.

We go into the classroom, where Rio is standing by a desk with shell-shocked eyes.

"How'd she take it?" asks Paulie.

Rio looks at him like that's the stupidest question he's ever heard. "Not so great." He takes a breath. "That went even worse than I thought it would."

Yesterday, after Rio told me how Catalina was blackmailing him, I made everyone else go home—which wasn't easy, because at that point I couldn't tell them why, and it was right before the pizza was supposed to get delivered, so Paulie was pretty mad. But Rio and I needed time to talk, alone. And after a lot of going around in circles about what to do, Rio finally decided he needed to get it out, right away, and tell Catalina it was over. So he left a message on her cell phone to meet him early at school. And I figured Monica and Paulie and I should be there to pick up the pieces, so this morning I told them everything.

Now here we are, and it's worse than I thought it would be, too. I don't much care about how Catalina took it, but Rio's face makes me think of the way Maddie looked once when she tried to get her bike past a neighbor's dog that was blocking the sidewalk and it turned right around and closed its jaws on her leg. There are times when you're just plain surprised by how much something hurts.

For Rio, the pain isn't over yet. "I saw Mr. Jaworski at the end of the hall," I tell him. "He's heading this way."

Rio looks around the room like he's thinking of hiding behind a desk or going through the window. "I can't do this. I can't tell him."

"Rio, you have to," says Paulie. I am *so* glad he and Monica are here right now. I've run out of words to argue with Rio, and I'm hoping that Paulie will find the right ones.

Paulie stares at Rio for a few seconds. "You still like Catalina and don't want to break up with her. Is that it?"

"No!" Rio snaps. His face has gone a bit red. "It's just, I mean, the whole thing is embarrassing. She was blackmailing me to be her boyfriend, and I went along with it. How pathetic does that sound?"

I guess there's no good answer to that, because none of us can find a word to answer him with right away.

"Look," Paulie says finally, "You can't let her get away with this."

Monica nods, setting her ponytail swinging. "He's right. She stole the software, and she lied, and she—"

"Okay," Rio stops her. "The thing is, if I tell Mr. Jaworski, it won't be just me getting in trouble. It'll be worse for her. She might get thrown out of school or something."

"And that would be bad because…?" Monica lets the question hang.

Rio pushes his bangs out of face and sighs again, a big defeated puff of breath. "I know. I get it. I have to do the right thing."

"And what's that?"

The voice makes all of us jump. It's Mr. Jaworski, standing in the doorway. No one remembered to keep watching out for him, so I don't know how long he's been there. His face doesn't give me any clue—he's not smiling but his eyes don't look mad.

I edge toward the door, waving at Paulie and Monica to follow, but Rio waves us back twice as hard.

"Don't go," he says, looking straight at me. And so we stay, witnesses to a conversation that I really don't want to hear.

"What's going on? Did the Chattercat stop chattering?" Mr. Jaworski asks lightly, and now it's clear to me he has no idea why we're here.

The room goes so quiet we should be able to hear each other breathe, except that we're all holding our breath, waiting for Rio to answer. Instead, we have to listen to the long, scratchy-whiney sound of Rio slowly unzipping his backpack. It seems like forever, the minutes stacking on top of each other, while Rio digs through all the books and papers and empty snack-size

Doritos bags, pretending to look for something that is probably in plain view, no matter how hard he tries not to see it.

Finally, right on the edge of "this is getting ridiculous," he pulls it from the backpack and holds it, arms extended, out to Mr. Jaworski: it's the box that holds all the disks for the stolen software.

I watch Mr. Jaworski. He knows right away what it is. And the look on his face is one I would never want aimed at me. It's not anger, because that's not his style. It's plain, simple, deep, complete disappointment.

"Rio, what are you doing with that?" says Mr. J. His voice is quiet and even, just like my dad's voice when he's trying not to explode after I've done something colossally stupid.

The silence spins out. I look back and forth between Mr. Jaworski and Rio.

Here's what I see in Mr. Jaworski: Along with the disappointment, there's surprise in his face too, like he can't believe Rio is really holding the software.

And Rio: His mouth is moving but no words are coming out. He's turning red again. I want to jump in but I know this is Rio's thing to face.

"I should have brought this back sooner," Rio blurts, pushing the box into Mr. Jaworski's hands. "I just didn't know what to do."

"So you're the one who took it?" asks Mr. J.

"No! I mean, I've had it, at my house, but I wasn't the one who stole it from here."

"And that would be…?" Mr. Jaworski turns and looks at Paulie, Monica, and me.

"No!" Rio says again. "They had nothing to do with it. Really, I swear that's true."

"Okay. So tell me who stole it. And why you have it now."

This is hurting Rio. Monica can see it too, because she lets out a tight little sigh and steps up to Mr. Jaworski.

"He doesn't want to get anyone in trouble," she says crisply. "But I don't mind doing it."

Paulie gives one of his snorts and points at Monica. "Yeah, Monica, you go, girl. Let the truth come out." I've forgotten how annoying Paulie can be sometimes, even without his twin around.

Monica goes on like she hasn't seen or heard him. "It was Catalina, Mr. J. She stole the software, and then she blackmailed Rio so he wouldn't tell anyone."

Mr. Jaworski's eyebrows go way up. He lays the box of software on his desk, slowly, like he needs to think before he says anything. Finally, he fixes Rio with another long stare. "Is that true, Rio?"

Rio nods, and even that small motion seems to make him miserable.

Mr. Jaworski sighs and looks at his watch. I know that look; I've seen my mom use it a million times. It means he knows this is a big mess and he's been pulled too deep into it to get out now and it's going to take a lot of work to fix it. And he hasn't even heard the whole story yet.

"Rio, I've got some time before my class gets here. I'll walk you to the principal's office and we'll start working this out."

Mr. J. puts a gentle hand on Rio's shoulder and steers him to the door. Start working this out, he said…well, we all know where that's heading: parents being called, long talks about actions and consequences, detentions, maybe suspensions. And I can't help feeling that I was the one who set in all in motion.

So it's weird that, as Rio heads into the hall and turns to give me a last glance, the look on his face isn't at all what I expected. The red-faced confusion, the misery—they're still there, but fading. What I focus on, instead, is the tiniest ghost of a smile.

There's a grating scrape from behind me as Paulie pulls out a chair. He drops into it with a gigantic sigh. "Oh, Rio, Rio, wherefore art thou such a spineless idiot?" he says, mangling Shakespeare again.

I turn on him, ready to gather up every ounce of tension that's been building inside me and let it go right in his face. Though Rio's made some mistakes, he doesn't deserve that.

But Paulie meets me with his hands in the air and a grin that shows all his teeth. "Whoa, cowgirl, just trying to lighten the mood. You looked ready to cry."

Monica fakes a kick in his direction, but somehow Paulie has managed to say exactly the right thing to pull me back to earth. I lift my chin and even manage a mirror of Rio's smile.

"You'll be fine," Monica says softly. "And so will Rio. But we still have some work to do." She nods toward the Chattercat, who's sitting on Mr. Jaworski's desk. Bella's bright blue plastic eyes point in our direction, as if she's been watching the whole scene play out. Which reminds me of Maddie, who sees and hears whatever is going on even when she can't talk about it.

Monica's right. We *do* still have work to do; it'll just be a little harder with Rio out of the picture. I grab Bella, sit down next to Paulie, and start pulling the Chattercat apart again. At least this is something we can really fix.

Paulie looks sideways at me. "Okay, so you didn't like spineless idiot. How about lovesick loser?"

This time I give him a full-watt smile. "Doesn't matter to me what you call him. A rose by any other name—"

"—is always gonna smell sweeter than Rio," he finishes for me. You can't top Paulie when it comes to messing up famous quotes. I'm just glad all that twisted brainpower is on my side.

# Twenty-Nine

# SADINA

When I was eight, Mom cut herself with a kitchen knife. It was an accident: she and Dad were both making dinner, and Mom got the job of slicing the onions. I remember her laughing because her eyes were watering so hard, and then in one slice of a second the knife took off a piece of her thumb.

She didn't stop laughing, like she didn't quite get right away that the blood on the cutting board was hers, but Dad picked up the phone—his hands still dripping water from washing a measuring cup—and dialed 911. I ran to the living room and watched for the ambulance out the front window. I couldn't hear a single noise from the kitchen, and I was too scared to go back and check what was going on. So I kept my cheek pressed to the glass and watched for the first pulse of red lights that would mean help was coming.

Now, six years later, Mom is in trouble again. This is trouble on a bigger scale—kind of like a five-car pile-up on the highway is bigger than a flat tire. Mom told me this morning that the meeting with the attorneys was bad. In fact, it couldn't have been worse. The lab director and all his lawyers believe *she* stole the research money, not Flynn, and they're pressing charges against her. And what that means is that my mother is going to be arrested.

The words sound crazy.

Things like this are not supposed to happen. But here I am again, too scared to think too hard about it, too scared to ask questions about what's going to happen next. Here I am again, in the living room with my cheek pressed to the glass, staring out the window. Except this time, calling 911 won't help. In fact, flashing lights are the last thing I want to see—because this time, it could be the signal that the police are here to take my mother away.

"This is it," Monica's voice comes from behind me.

I turn away from the window and sit down next to her on the sofa. Monica is here, and Paulie is here, because we've just given Maddie the latest, fixed-up version of Bella the Chattercat that we finished today at school. Last time I gave the cat to Maddie, I didn't want anyone else around. This time, I couldn't stand to be by myself. Because we've finally run out of time. This is our last chance. If the Chattercat doesn't work, or if Maddie still won't talk to it, then there's nothing else I can do to help Mom.

Mom and Dad are waiting here with us. They know what Monica and Paulie and Rio and I (and Catalina too, to be fair) have done, and they're grateful for it. But there's not much hope on their faces, neither of them quite believing, I think, that help could come from a seven-year-old kid and a souped-up robot cat.

I can't sit still another second. I start pacing in front of the sofa, up to the bookcase, over to the window and back again. I'm driving Monica crazy, I'm sure, but she won't say a thing. She knows I'm trying to stay one step ahead of all the ugly scared thoughts in my head.

I'm concentrating so hard on nothing that I pass by the window two times before I actually look up and see them: two black-and-white patrol cars parked at the curb in front of the house. I don't know how they got there. They must have come quietly, without lights or sirens. They slid by, catching me when I wasn't watching, to take my mother away.

Maybe I've squeezed my eyes shut, because for a second my world goes black. Maybe I speak, but I never hear a sound. Maybe my knees buckle, because in the next instant Monica and Paulie are by my side, each with an arm around me, and I know I wouldn't be standing if they weren't there.

Then the doorbell rings, and the noise to me is as loud as sirens, cracking me back into sight and sound and action.

I whip around to look for Mom. She's already on her feet, her hand in Dad's, and her chin up high. Even in this moment, knowing that when she opens the front door her life will change forever, she looks right at me with nothing but love and strength. It's a gift she's handing me, a piece of herself, like giving away your climber's rope when you're the one who has to scale the cliff.

"I'm not done yet," I tell her.

I've whispered the words and I don't think she hears me, but Paulie and Monica do. They look at me together. They're not ready to give up either. So when I start talking, it's like this is a play we've rehearsed once before, giving each other directions and feeding each other lines that somehow we already know.

"We need time," I say, watching Mom and Dad head out of the living room toward the front hall. "Can you stall them?"

"Stall the cops?" Paulie grins, like I've just handed him a free all-day pass to an amusement park. "My pleasure."

"Stall the cops?" Monica echoes. "How's that supposed to happen?"

"Absolutely no idea." Paulie grabs her arm and heads after my parents. "Think fast. We have about five seconds to come up with a plan."

And I have about that much time to get to Maddie and see if the Chattercat worked. I'm out of the living room right on the heels of Paulie and Monica, but I cut left and head up the stairs. I'm moving so fast I'm not even sure my feet are touching the ground.

When I reach Maddie's room I come to a dead stop. The door is closed. It's supposed to be that way. It's supposed to *stay* that way until Maddie is ready to come out on her own. I didn't want anyone watching and listening and scaring Maddie with the realization of how much this matters.

But even now I can hear voices from the front hall. There's a low, calm voice I don't know, then a rapid-fire spray of words tumbling over each other that must be coming from Monica and Paulie, spilling out whatever story they came up with in the space of five seconds.

I need to know—*now*—if the Chattercat worked. If it really got Maddie to talk about the night of the break-in. And if she really saw Flynn.

But I don't want to open Maddie's door. Because then I'll get the answers to all those *ifs*. And they may not be the answers I'm hoping for.

# Thirty

# MADDIE

"**W**hat happened the night you stopped talking?"

Maddie stands at her bedroom window, as far away from Bella as she can possibly get. She doesn't want to turn around and face the question on the glowing blue screen that's connected to Bella. Maddie knows the cat's bright eyes are staring at her, waiting for an answer.

Outside the sunset is turning the edge of the sky a dusty pink. Pretty soon it will be dark. Too dark to pretend any more that she's looking out the window.

It's funny, for so long Maddie has wanted nothing more than to talk with Bella. Now it's finally happening—but it isn't turning out the way she imagined. Bella is making her think about things she wants to forget. It isn't fair. For the first time she can remember, Maddie is mad at Bella. Mad enough to turn her back and ignore the cat who's supposed to be her best friend.

But here's the thing. If she stops talking to Bella, maybe Bella will stop talking to her.

The thought makes Maddie swallow hard.

Slowly she swivels around. Bella is sitting on the nightstand next to her bed. Maddie crosses the room and sinks down onto the rug in front of the nightstand. She looks into Bella's face. Bella looks right back at her, like nothing else in the world matters. Maddie reaches out to stroke Bella's head.

"I remember what happened," Maddie whispers. "But I don't want to say it."

Bella tips her head to the side, and another question comes up on the screen. "Why don't you want to say it?"

"It scared me."

"It's hard when things scare you."

"Yeah," Maddie sighs. "Do you get scared too?"

"Everybody gets scared sometimes."

"Not everybody. Not Sadina. She would have told everybody."

"You don't have to tell everybody. You can tell me."

That's true. Maddie can tell Bella anything.

From the door comes the sound of three soft knocks. Someone wants to come in here. But Maddie doesn't answer. She wants to get out the words that have been stuck in her throat and give them to Bella.

"It was dark and I was so scared. I didn't even want to look. But I couldn't help it. He was there and I saw him."

The knocks come again, louder. Still Maddie ignores them.

"I don't know why he was here, Bella. He shouldn't have been here."

"Who shouldn't have been here, Maddie?"

"It was—" Maddie takes in a deep breath.

Whoever is outside her room can't wait: the door swings open. It's Sadina, her hair falling out of her ponytail and her face looking like it does when her basketball team is losing a game. She runs across the room, skids to a stop and falls to her knees in front of Maddie, grabbing her shoulders.

And Maddie—who hasn't been able to talk to Sadina or Mom or Dad or anyone for so long—is finally able to let it all go.

"It was Flynn. He didn't want me to tell anyone. He made me promise not to." Maddie looks up at Sadina. "Is it okay to tell?"

In answer Sadina leans in to Maddie, forehead to forehead. Sadina's eyes look wet, and she's gripping Maddie's shoulders so tightly it hurts.

"Yes. It's okay. It's exactly the right thing to do."

# Thirty-One

# SADINA

"**I** have proof."

I'm standing in front of the police officers with Bella in my hands, blocking their way out my front door. One of them, the one with the low, calm voice, is holding my mother's elbow, which makes me want to either scream or cry— I'm not sure which. He looks at me patiently, like I'm an irritation but he's decided not to be mean about it.

"I have to ask you to step out of the way," he says evenly, with a quick look at my dad that sends the message, *it would be a good idea to move her.*

"You have to *listen*," I say. My voice cracks, and now it's definite—the tears are going to win. "It's all true. Maddie saw Flynn in our house. She said he broke in and took his phone out of my mom's desk. The cat recorded everything Maddie said."

As soon as those last words are out of my mouth, I realize how ridiculous they sound.

I look toward Monica and Paulie, though I can't fairly expect any more help from them. When I came flying down the stairs from Maddie's room, they were just finishing up the story that was meant to stall the cops. The crazy part is, the story they decided to use was the truth. The truth about Maddie's selective mutism, about how she stopped talking, about how we programmed her favorite robot cat to open her up again. But Officer Calm-Voice is not buying it.

"Sadina, honey…" Dad steps toward me and I step backward, holding Bella out like a shield.

Instead of backing into open air, I hit something solid, something that gives a grunt and smells like Sword aftershave.

Rio.

I don't dare turn my head around but I know it's him. The question is…how? He's supposed to be grounded until his parents "can trust him again"—in other words, another decade or so. But somehow he's here. And he's got my back.

"Officer Angelo," he says—I'm wondering how he got to know a member of the Springfield police force well enough to remember his name, until I realize, of course, they have name tags—and when everyone looks Rio's way he goes on. "Sadina's telling the truth about the robot. And I've brought someone who can explain how it works."

Okay, now I have to turn around. There's Rio, bangs half over his face, looking at me with his half-smile. And behind him…I can't believe it's Mr. Jaworski.

I'm standing there, stunned, and I don't even realize my mouth is hanging open until Mr. Jaworski looks at me and smiles too.

"It's Mr. J," says Paulie. "J for just-in-time."

Yeah, kind of too perfectly timed to be coincidence. I turn back to Paulie and Monica, who aren't looking surprised at all.

Monica holds up her cell phone and mouths the words "text message." Oh. So there was more to their five-minute on-the-run plan than I realized. They got Rio—and he got Mr. Jaworski. I guess they figured it out a step ahead of me: this is one game we can't hope to win without the whole team.

Mr. Jaworski gently nudges me to one side and comes past me into the house.

"If you can give me just a minute or two, Officer Angelo," he says, "I can tell you what these kids have been up to. Some amazing design work. And that cat"—he points at Bella and grins—"I think you'll agree it's worth listening to what it has to say."

Officer Angelo looks at his partner, raises his eyebrows, and lets go of Mom's arm.

Next thing I know we're all back in the living room, ten people piled all over the sofa and chairs, perched on the windowsill and the coffee table. I'm sitting as close to Mom as I can get, and Maddie—she's here now too—is tight against my other side, not talking but nodding like a little bobble-head as everyone lays the story out one more time, words sliding past each other and sometimes bunching into piles, but somehow the two cops seem to make sense of it all.

And when we're done, what happens is this: Mom still has to go with them to the police station.

But she's not under arrest. Officer Angelo just wants to interview her about the break-in and all the money that got stolen from the company and how Flynn was involved. That's going to be tough for Mom. To her, their years of friendship count for something. She can't toss that away as easily as Flynn did. But she'll tell the truth. And after that, I think things won't look so good for Flynn.

Bella is going along with Mom as evidence. I watch Maddie's face as she hears that. There are about a dozen different ways it could have gone, but in the end she can't hold back the excitement that Bella is so important. That her own words were so important.

And it's true. Between the two of them, Maddie and Bella, they were Mom's ticket back home.

# Thirty-Two

## SADINA

"I was thinking," I begin.

"Yeah, got that," says Paulie, "from the way your forehead was all wrinkled up, like it hurt."

I send a look his way that he ignores completely. But I'm not really mad. Paulie doesn't irritate me quite as much as he used to.

We're sitting on the steps of my front porch, waiting for Mrs. Walker to show up and get Rio, since he really is grounded and not supposed to go anywhere. She was okay with bending the rules and letting him come here to help keep my mom from getting arrested, but now he's got to go home and do his own time.

It's dark out, and a bit cold, but none of us—Rio and Paulie and Monica and me—seem to mind.

"This," I start again, "is what I was thinking. Remember what Mrs. Weber said in class last week, when we were talking about Romeo and Juliet? Something about how maybe they could have made other choices, so things would have ended differently? You know, without dead bodies all around."

Monica sees right away where I'm heading. "Right. So you think we might have had other choices too?"

That's it. Like maybe I should have talked to Rio sooner—much sooner—about that stupid software and he wouldn't have gotten in so much trouble. And maybe Mom should have reported Flynn sooner, right after she heard his brother's message on his phone, and she wouldn't have ended up nearly going to jail herself. The trouble is, the choices are never that easy or that clear when you're in the middle of them. And figuring out the right thing to do, well, that's like finding a clean T-shirt under a pile of laundry in my room: there's a lot of other stuff to dig through.

A pair of headlights comes around the corner down the street. Rio's mother is here.

Rio gets up and stretches. "Back to house arrest. Don't forget that I exist."

As if. I follow Rio off the porch. Halfway to the car, I realize it's pretty dark out here: a moonless, starless night. I can't see Monica or Paulie behind us. And I'm pretty sure they can't see us. I grab Rio's hand and he looks back at me. I don't stop to think it through or decide if it's the right choice. I just lean forward and kiss him.

I don't hang around to see his reaction. I turn right around and head back to the house.

Maddie is waiting for me at the bottom of the steps. She gives me her angel face and wraps her arms around me in a tight hug. I try to hug her back but she's done with that. She says in a voice that's perfectly loud and clear, "I just saw you kiss Rio."

So I guess she's really starting to talk again. First to Bella. Then to me. Then right in front of my best friends.

And that's a good thing.

Right?

# THE END

You just finished reading my story —

but now I need YOUR help!

Rio, Monica, Paulie and I — and yeah, Catalina too — are getting caught up in a lot more TROUBLE....

Midnight, in the dark, in the rain, Rio shows up at my door — and you WON'T BELIEVE what happened to his brain.

Then, on a spidery, spooky Halloween, I end up stuck with Catalina...at the bottom of a pit below a very HAUNTED house.  You've got to get me out of there!

As fast as you can, go to

www.throughmywindow.org

I'll meet you there!

Sadina